Players

"Don DeLillo . . . is original, versatile, and, in his disdain of last year's emotional guarantees, fastidious. . . . Into our technology-ridden daily lives he reads the sinister ambiguities, the floating ugliness of America's recent history."—John Updike, *The New Yorker*

"Lyrical, romantic and absorbing. . . . What matters in [*Players*] is the peripheral movement, a surrealistic swirl of terrorism, anomie and sex, into which the central characters and the reader alike are ultimately consumed."—Ardie Ivie, *The Los Angeles Times*

"A hard-edged, chilling work by an important American writer."
—William J. Harding, *The Philadelphia Inquirer*

"Few recent novels have found so admirably congruent a form for their subject. . . . It is a measure of DeLillo's bravura that he tries [to look grandly at the whole state of things], and a measure of his art that, for all his deceptive simplicity, he succeeds."
—Diane Johnson, front page, *The New York Times Book Review*

"The novel's central themes are important and relevant; DeLillo's handling of them is responsible and suggestive; the characters represent a wide range of intellectual positions and psychological sets; and as always the writing is remarkably good."—J.D. O'Hara, *The Nation*

"DeLillo may be our wittiest writer."
—John Leonard, *The New York Times*

"It would be too easy to say that DeLillo is satirizing modern, thrill-seeking amoral urban life. What he does is to convey its chill and terror. Every so often some bottom drops out and there are real people, not just players, desperate to lead meaningful lives."
—Joan Joffe Hall, *The Houston Post*

Players

PLAYERS

by

Don DeLillo

VINTAGE BOOKS

A Division of Random House
New York

First Vintage Books Edition, May 1984
Copyright © 1977 by Don DeLillo
All rights reserved under International and Pan-American
Copyright Conventions. Published in the United States by
Random House, Inc., New York, and simultaneously in
Canada by Random House of Canada Limited, Toronto.
Originally published by Alfred A. Knopf, Inc. in 1977.

Portions of this book have
previously appeared in *Esquire*.

Library of Congress Cataloging in Publication Data
DeLillo, Don.
Players.
Originally published: New York : Knopf, 1977.
I. Title.
[PS 3554.E4425P55 1984]   813'.54   83-40312
ISBN 0-394-72382-1 (pbk.)

Manufactured in the United States of America

Players

The Movie

Someone says: "Motels. I like motels. I wish I owned a chain, worldwide. I'd like to go from one to another to another. There's something self-realizing about that."

The lights inside the aircraft go dim. In the piano bar everyone is momentarily still. It's as though they're realizing for the first time how many systems of mechanical and electric components, what exact management of stresses, power units, consolidated thrust and energy it has taken to reduce their sensation of flight to this rudimentary tremble. Beyond the windows not a nuance of sunset remains. Four men, three women inhabit this particular frame of arrested motion. The only sound is drone. One second of darkness, all we've had thus far, has been enough to intensify the implied bond which, more than distance, speed or destination, makes each journey something of a mystery to be worked out by the combined talents of the travelers, all gradually aware of each other's code of recognition. In the cabin just ahead, the meal is over, the movie is about to begin.

As light returns, the man seated at the piano begins to play a tune. Standing nearby is a woman, shy of thirty, light-haired and unhappy about flying. There's a man to her left, holding the rim of his drinking glass against his lower lip. They're clearly together, a couple, wearing each other.

The stewardess moves past with pillows and magazines, glancing into the cabin at the movie screen, credits super-imposed on a still image of a deserted golf course, early light. Near the entrance to the piano bar, about a dozen feet from the piano itself, are two chairs separated by an ashtray stand. Another obvious couple sits here, men in this case. Both look at the piano player, anticipating their own delight at whatever pointed comment his choice of tunes is meant to suggest.

The third woman sits near the rear of the compartment. She pops cashew nuts into her mouth and washes them down with ginger ale. She's in her early forties, indifferently dressed. We know nothing else about her.

Without headsets, of course, the people in the piano bar aren't able to hear the sound track of the movie being shown. Early light, some haze, surfaces burnished with moisture. As the final credit disappears, the flag marking a distant green lifts slightly and ripples and then men appear, golfers and their paraphernalia, at the left edge of the screen.

Feeling his way, still tentative in these introductory mo-ments, the pianist is rendering a typical score for a silent film. This amuses the others, although their smiles and expressions aren't directed toward anyone in particular but are instead allowed to drift, as happens among travelers in the initial stages. The stewardess alone seems disappointed by the limits of this logical association between music and film. True, the movie they're viewing is in effect a silent one. But she gives the impression she's been through this routine before.

Between the piano bar and the screen, the rows of seats appear to be empty, the top of not a single head visible over the high-backed mechanical chairs. We assume people are sitting there, motionless, content to sift among the images.

The woman near the piano begins to yawn, almost compulsively, a mild attack of something. She yawns on planes just as she used to yawn (adolescence) seconds before getting on a roller coaster, or (young womanhood) when she was dialing her father's phone number. Her companion, with a stylized jerkiness that's appropriately Chaplinesque in nature, brings his left foot way up behind him and boots her lightly in the rear, an act so neatly conceived it makes her laugh in mid-yawn.

The golfers plod onscreen, seven or eight in all, white, male, portly, several driving golf carts, bumping slowly over knolls in single file. They're all middle-aged and wear the kind of rampantly bright sports clothes that suburban men favor on weekends, colors so strident they might serve as illustrations of the folly of second childhood.

The piano player adds an element of suspense to his sequence. His face, although lined about the eyes, has been slow to lose an appealing openness, the objective emblem of a moral competence we associate with young people who make pottery or do oceanic research.

Moist surfaces, light breeze, the mist beginning to clear. The golfers cluster around a tee and the members of an improvised threesome drive in turn, twisting their bodies to the flight of the ball. They set off down the fairway as their companions take practice swings, one of them (yellow cardigan) tucking the club head into his armpit and sighting along the shaft, briefly, in a rifle-firing jest, this wholly offhand moment shading away into borders of surrounding activity.

The older of the homosexuals leans over the top of the ashtray to give his companion a theatrical nudge. The piano player has also noted the nearly concealed gesture of the golfer in the yellow cardigan and responds with a series of bass chords. Import, foreboding.

It's worthwhile to point out that the characters and landscape are being seen through the special viewpoint of a long lens. This is a lesson in the intimacy of distance. Space in this context seems less an intuitive experience than a series of relative densities. It intervenes in compact blocks. What the camera shares with those watching is an appreciation of optical cunning. The sense of being unseen. The audience as privileged onlookers.

The piano music, a substitute sound track as well as a medium of autonomous comment, begins to express a deepening degree of (sly) apprehension that blends well with the film's precisely timed sequence of shots, each slightly briefer than the one before, a suggestion of routine events about to give way to some unforeseen pressure.

The young woman has managed to stop yawning. The man alongside studies the fingernails of his right hand. He does this with fingers bent in over the palm, thumb extended. The woman, without taking her eyes from the screen, reaches over, grabs his thumb and begins to bend it back. He looks up and away, eyeballs rolling. In time he begins making the sound either or both of them make when troubled by anxiety, critical choices, nameless dread, the prospect of boring dinner guests, his job, her job. The woman in the rear looks on without expression. It's a prolonged hum, the speech sound *m*.

The golfers on this sweet green morning attend to their game. Together again momentarily on a particular fairway they appear almost to be posing in massed corporate glory before a distant flag. It is now that the vigilant hidden thing, the special consciousness implicit in a long lens, is made to show itself.

A man, his back to the camera, rises from the underbrush in the immediate foreground, about two hundred yards from the golfers. When he turns to signal to someone, it's evident he holds a weapon in his right hand, a semiautomatic rifle. After signaling he doesn't reassume his crouch. One of the golfers selects an iron.

Another man comes up out of the shrubbery, rising to his full height. We don't know his precise location as it relates to any of the other people. He faces the camera. Behind him are deep woods. His clothing is diverse—baseball cap (peak up), threadbare paisley vest, work shirt, garrison belt, white trousers fitted into high boots. Bandoliers crisscross his chest. He carries a cut-down Enfield.

The long lens picks out a man and woman standing at the top of a small hill. More bass chords. Accumulating doom. At this distance they appear to be built into the sky, motionless, both carrying rifles. Another woman, in a much tighter shot, stands alone in a sand trap, barefoot, wearing a tank top and fringed buckskin pants. One leg is bent, all her weight on the other, the left. She holds a machete back up over her right shoulder, resting it there.

The piano player moves to the end of the bench and sits up on one haunch for a fuller look at the screen, his fingers not straying from the keyboard. The first of the terrorists begins the long run across the fairway.

Most of what happens next takes place in slow motion. The terrorists are seen running, one by one, out into the open and toward the golfers. Being young, and dressed as they are in jeans and leather and attic regalia, and running, they can hardly fail to be a lyrical interlude. The subnormal speed at which their bodies perform makes them seem creatures of gravity, near animals struggling toward some fundamental transition, their incomparable crude beauty a result of carefully detailed physical stress. On the hill a single figure remains, man, hands in pockets, shotgun under one arm.

The first runner starts firing as he approaches the group. A man in a sweater falls, golf balls rolling out of his pockets. The terrorists, trying to isolate their victims singly or in twos, have three men dead almost immediately. Bodies tumble in slow motion. There's blood on golf bags, on white shoes, spreading over tartan pants. Several men try to run. One swings his club and is shot in the groin by the man with the Enfield. He topples into a pond, clouding it with blood. The stewardess serves mixed drinks to the male couple and a ginger ale to the woman in the rear.

It isn't until now that the silent-movie music reveals the extent of its true relationship to the events on the screen. To the glamour of revolutionary violence, to the secret longing it evokes in the most docile soul, the piano's shiny tinkle brings an irony too apt to be ignored. The simple innocence of this music undermines the photogenic terror, reducing it to an empty swirl.

We're prompted to remember something here, although this act of recall may be more mythic than subjective, a spool of Biograph dreams. It flows through us. Upright pianos in a thousand nickelodeons. Heart-throbbing romance and knockabout comedy and nerve-racking suspense. History this weightless has an easy time of it, we learn, contending with the burdens of the present day.

In the piano bar the small audience laughs, except for the woman drinking ginger ale. Despite the camera's fascination for the lush slaughter of these clearly expendable men, the scene becomes confused, due to the melodramatic piano. We're steeped in gruesomely humorous ambiguity, a spectacle of ridiculous people doing awful things to total fools.

What conceivably makes this even funnier (to some) is the nature of the game itself. Golf. That anal round of scrupulous caution and petty griefs. Watching golfers being massacred, to trills and other ornaments, seems to strike those in the piano bar, at any rate, as an occasion for sardonic delight.

Bodies are blown back into sand and high grass. If it's all a little bit like cowboys and Indians, so much the better. One of the golfers tries to escape in his cart, steering it toward the woods. The young woman with the machete sets out in pursuit, arms pumping in slow motion, hair sailing out.

The piano player introduces a chase theme. His mock-boyish face carefully qualifies every smile—a grimace here, a shudder there. The violence, after all, is expert and intense. His fellow passengers laugh as the golf cart overturns on a slope and the woman skids down after it, her arm slowly raising to deliver a backhanded slash. The man tries to crawl away. She walks calmly alongside, chopping at his back and neck. Here the chase music gives way to a lighthearted lament.

The woman leaves the machete in his body and heads back to the others.

The man who'd remained on the hill walks down now into this scene of fresh death. He is liberation's bright angel, in watch cap and black slicker, coming out of the sun. He wears lampblack under his eyes and thick white pigment across his forehead and cheeks. The others stand around, taking deep breaths, consciously intent on nothing but their own exalted fatigue. He holds the shotgun out away from him, as nearly parallel to his body as he can feasibly manage, muzzle up. The golfers are strewn everywhere. We see them frame by frame, split open, little packages of lacquer. The terrorist chief, *jefe,* honcho, leader fires several rounds into the air—a blood rite or passionate declaration. Buster Keaton, says the piano.

And now the stewardess serves drinks to those who need them and everybody gradually moves to different parts of the piano bar, their loss of interest in the movie manifesting itself in this nearly systematic restlessness. With the configuration thus upset, the piano silent, the film ignored, there is a sense of feelings turning inward. They remember they are on a plane, travelers. Their true lives lie below, even now beginning to reassemble themselves, calling this very flesh out of the air, in mail waiting to be opened, in telephones ringing and paper work on office desks, in the chance utterance of a name.

ONE

1

The man was often there, standing outside Federal Hall, corner of Wall and Nassau. Lean and gray-stubbled, maybe sev-
enty, sweating brightly in a frayed shirt and slightly overused
suit, he held a homemade sign over his head, sometimes for
whole afternoons, lowering his arms only long enough to
allow blood to recirculate. The sign was two by three feet,
hand-lettered on both sides, political in nature. Loungers at
this hour, most of them sitting on the steps outside the Hall,
were too distracted by the passers-by to give the man and his
sign—familiar sights, after all—more than a cursory glance.
Down here, in the district, men still assembled solemnly to
gape at females. Working in a roar of money, they felt, gave
them that vestigial right.

Lyle stood at the door of a restaurant, cleaning his fingernails with the toothpick he'd lifted from the little bowl when
he paid the check. He no longer ate in the Exchange luncheon
club, pleasant as it was, restricted to members and their guests,
well run and comfortably appointed as it was, so capable the
waiters, knowing one's name, so effortless the attentions of the

washroom personnel, swift with towels, brilliant in the understated brushing of one's suit, actual blacks, convenient as it
was, an elevator ride from the trading floor itself. He watched
the old man standing in the sun, arms upright, one hand trembling. Then he moved into the lunchtime crowds, wondering if
he'd somehow become too complex to enjoy a decent meal in
attractive surroundings, served, a minute from the floor, by
reasonably cheerful men.

Across Broadway, a few blocks north, Pammy stood in the
sky lobby of the south tower of the World Trade Center, fight-
ing the crowd that was pushing her away from an express
elevator going down. She wanted to go down, although she
worked on the eighty-third floor, because she was in the wrong
building. This was the second time she'd come back from
lunch and entered the south tower instead of the north. She
would have to fight the lunch-hour mob in the sky lobby here,
go down to the main floor, walk over to the north tower, take
the express up to *that* seventy-eighth-floor sky lobby, fight
more crowds, then take a local to eighty-three, panels vibrat-
ing. Trying to move sideways now, she realized someone
nearby was staring into her face.

"It's Pam, isn't it?"

"I don't, what."

"Jeanette."

"Actually no."

"High school."

"Jeanette."

"How many years was that ago?"

"High school, Jeanette."

"I don't blame you not remembering. Boy, the time."

"I think I may remember now."

"You work here, right? Everybody works here."

"I'm supposed to be on the down."

"You're still remembering? Jeanette, who hung around with Theresa and Geri."

"I remembered just then."

"That was how many years, right?"

"They won't let me on."

"But don't you love this place? You should see how I have to get to the cafeteria. A local and an express down. Then an express up. Then the escalator if you can get there without them ripping your flesh to pieces."

"Torn asunder, I know."

"You work for the state, being here?"

"I'm in the wrong tower."

Pammy and Lyle didn't go out much anymore. They used to spend a lot of time discovering restaurants. They traveled to the palest limits of the city, eating in little river warrens near the open approaches to bridges or in family restaurants out in the boroughs, the neutral décor of such places and their remoteness serving as tokens of authenticity. They went to clubs where new talent auditioned and comic troupes improvised. On spring weekends they bought plants at greenhouses in the suburbs and went to boatyards on City Island or the North Shore to help friends get their modest yachts seaworthy. Gradually their range diminished. Even movies, double features in the chandeliered urinals of upper Broadway, no longer tempted them. What seemed missing was the desire to compile.

They had sandwiches for dinner, envelopes of soup, or went

around the corner to a coffee shop, eating quickly while a man mopped the floor near their table, growling like a jazz bassist. There was a Chinese place three blocks away. This was as far as they traveled, most evenings and weekends, for nonutilitarian purposes. Pammy was skilled at distinguishing among the waiters here. A source of quiet pride.

Lyle passed time watching television. Sitting in near darkness about eighteen inches from the screen, he turned the channel selector every half minute or so, sometimes much more frequently. He wasn't looking for something that might sustain his interest. Hardly that. He simply enjoyed jerking the dial into fresh image-burns. He explored content to a point. The tactile-visual delight of switching channels took precedence, however, transforming even random moments of content into pleasing territorial abstractions. Watching television was for Lyle a discipline like mathematics or Zen. Commercials, station breaks, Spanish-language dramas had more to offer as a rule than standard programming. The repetitive aspect of commercials interested him. Seeing identical footage many times was a test for the resourcefulness of the eye, its ability to re-select, to subdivide an instant of time. He rarely used sound. Sound was best served by those UHF stations using faulty equipment or languages other than English.

Occasionally he watched one of the public-access channels. There was an hour or so set aside every week for locally crafted pornography, the work of native artisans. He found on the screen a blunter truth certainly than in all that twinkling flesh in the slick magazines. He sat in his bowl of curved space, his dusty light. There was a child's conspicuous immodesty in all this genital aggression. People off the streets looking for something to suck. Hand-held cameras searching out the odd crotch. Lyle was immobile through this sequence of small gray bodies. What he saw retained his attention completely even as it continued to dull his senses. The hour seemed like four. Weary as he was, blanked out, bored by all these posturing desperadoes, he could easily have watched through the night, held by the mesh effect of television, the electrostatic glow that seemed a privileged state between wave and visual image, a secret of celestial energy. He wondered if he'd become too complex to look at naked bodies, as such, and be stirred.

"Here, look. We're here, folks. The future has collapsed right in on us. And what does it look like?"

"You made me almost jump."

"It looks like this. It looks like waves and waves of static. It's being beamed in ahead of schedule, which accounts for the buzzing effect. It looks like seedy people from Mercer Street."

"Let me sleep, hey."

"See, look, I'm saying. Just as I speak. I mean it's this. We're sitting watching in the intimacy and comfort of our bedroom and they've got their loft and their camera and it gets shown because that's the law. As soon as they see a camera they take off their clothes. It used to be people waved."

"Good."

"Right here. Ri'chere, ladies and gennemen. See the pandas play with their shit. Triffic, triffic."

Pammy had the kind of smile that revealed a trace of upper gum. She'd been told that was touching. In her more complicated movements, in package-carrying or the skirting of derelicts, she showed a gawkiness that was like a clap of hands

bringing back her youth. She had a narrow face, hair lank
and moderately blond. People liked her eyes. Some presence in
them seemed at times to jump out in greeting. She was animated in conversation, a waver of hands, an interrupter, head
going, eyes intent on the speaker's mouth, her own lips sometimes repeating the beat. Her body was firm and straight and
could have been that of a swimmer. Sometimes she didn't associate herself with it.

She worked for a firm called the Grief Management Coun-
cil. Grief was not the founder's name; it referred to intense
mental suffering, deep remorse, extreme anguish, acute sorrow
and the like. The number of employees varied, sometimes
radically, from month to month. In its brochures, which
Pammy wrote, Grief Management was described as a large
and growing personal-services organization whose clinics,
printed material and trained counselors served the community
in its efforts to understand and assimilate grief. There were
fees for individuals, group fees, special consultation terms,
charges for booklets and teaching aids, payments for family
sessions and marital grief seminars. Most regional offices were
small and located in squat buildings that also housed surgical-
supply firms and radiology labs. These buildings were usually
the first of a planned complex that never materialized. Pammy
had visited several, for background, and the photos she took
for her brochures had to be severely cropped to eliminate the
fields of weeds and bulldozed earth. It was her original view
that the World Trade Center was an unlikely headquarters for
an outfit such as this. But she changed her mind as time
passed. Where else would you stack all this grief? Somebody
anticipated that people would one day crave the means to

codify their emotions. A clerical structure would be needed. Teams of behaviorists assembled in the sewers and conceived a brand of futurism based on filing procedures. To Pammy the towers didn't seem permanent. They remained concepts, no less transient for all their bulk than some routine distortion of light. Making things seem even more fleeting was the fact that office space at Grief Management was constantly being reapportioned. Workmen sealed off some areas with partitions, opened up others, moved out file cabinets, wheeled in chairs and desks. It was as though they'd been directed to adjust the amount of furniture to levels of national grief.

Pammy shared a partitioned area with Ethan Segal, who was responsible for coordinating the activities of the regional offices. Because of his longish hair, his repertoire of ruined flourishes, his extravagantly shabby clothing, a somewhat ironic overrefinement of style, Pammy thought of him as semi-Edwardian. Even the signs he showed of middle age were tinged with a kind of blithe ornamentation. Extra weight gave him an airiness, as it does some people, and Ethan used this illusion of buoyancy to appear nonchalant while walking, lofty in conversation, a coward at games. And those sweeping motions of his arms, the ruined flourishes, became more dramatic, emptier (by intention), as various irregularities crept into his posture. With him lived Jack Laws, a would-be drifter. Jack had a patch of pure white at the back of an otherwise dark head of hair. His success with certain people was based largely on this genetic misconjecture. It was the mark, the label, the stamp, the sign, the emblem of something mysterious.

"Adorable useless Jack."

"What, I'm working."

"It's amazing, it's almost supernatural, really, the way people get an idea, a tiny human hankering for something, and it becomes a way of life, the obsession of the ages. To me this is amazing. A person like me. Nurtured on realities, the limitations of things."

"I walked in the wrong tower."

"Jack wants to live in Maine."

"I find that, you know, why not?"

"It's the driving force of his life, suddenly, out of nowhere, this thing, Maine, this word, which is all it is, since he's never been there."

"But it's a good word," she said.

"Maine."

"Maine," she said. "It's simple maybe, Ethan, but it has a strength to it. You feel it's the sort of core, the moral core."

"This from a person who uses words, so it must mean something."

"I use words, absolutely."

"So maybe Jack has something."

"Ethan, Jack always has something. Whatever it is, Jack has the inner meanings of it, the pure parts. We both know this about Jack."

"What do I do, commute?"

"I'd like to be there now," she said. "This city. Time of year."

"July, August."

"Scream city."

"You think he's got something then."

"I use words."

"You think he's picked a good one."

"Jack has. Jack always has."

In the same way that she thought of Ethan as semi-Edwardian, she considered his mouth, apart from the rest of him, as German. He had assertive lips, something of a natural sneer, and there were times when he nearly drooled while laughing, bits of fizz appearing at the corners of his mouth. These were things Pammy associated with scenes of the German high command in World War II movies.

"Maybe we'll go up and look."

"Look at what?" she said.

"The terrain. Get the feel of it. Just to see. He's telling everyone. Maine or else. Not that I'd commute, obviously. But just to see. Three or four weeks. He'll get it out of his system and we'll come back. Life as before, the same old grind."

"Maine."

"You're right, you know, Pammy old kid. It does have a kind of hewn strength. Sort of unbreakable, unlike Connecticut. I like hearing it."

"Maine."

"Say it, say it."

"Maine," she said. "Maine."

Lyle saw his number on the enunciator board. He went to one of the booths along the south wall, reaching for the phone extended by a clerk.

"Buy five thousand Motors at sixty-five."

"GM."

"There's more behind it."

He put down the phone and walked over to post 3. An old friend, McKechnie, crossed toward him at an angle. They

passed without sign of recognition. Sporadically over the next
several hours, as Lyle moved to different parts of the floor,
traded in the garage annex, conversed with people at his
booth, he thought of something that hadn't entered his mind in
a great many years. It was the feeling that everyone knew his
thoughts. He couldn't recall when this suspicion had first occurred to him. Very early on, obviously. Everyone knew his
thoughts but he didn't know any of theirs. People on the floor
were moving more quickly now. An electric cross-potential
was in the air, a nearly headlong sense of revel and woe. On
the board an occasional price brought noise from the floor
brokers, the specialists, the clerks. Lyle watched the stock
codes and the stilted figures below them, the computer spew.
Inner sex crimes. A fancywork of violence and spite. Those
were the shames of his adolescence. If everyone here knew
his present thoughts, if that message in greenish cipher that
moved across the board represented the read-outs of Lyle
Wynant, it would be mental debris alone that caused him
humiliation, all the unwordable rubble, the glass, rags and
paper of his tiny indefinable manias. The conversations he had
with himself, straphanging in a tunnel. All the ceremonial patterns, the soul's household chores. These were far more reveal-
ing, he believed, than some routine incest variation. There
was more noise from the floor as Xerox appeared on the
board. Male and female messengers flirted in transit. The
paper waste accumulated. It was probably not an uncommon
feeling among older children and adolescents that everyone
knows your thoughts. It put you at the center of things, although in a passive and frightening way. *They know but do
not show it.* When things slowed down he went to the smoking

area just beyond post 1. Frank McKechnie was in there, field-stripping a cigarette.

"I'm in no mood."

"Neither am I."

"It's total decay."

"What are we talking about?" Lyle said.

"The outside world."

"Is it still there? I thought we'd effectively negated it. I thought that was the upshot."

"I'm walking around seeing death masks. This, that, the other. My wife is having tests. They take tissue from underneath the arm. My brother is also out there with his phone calls. I'm seeing visions, Lyle."

"Don't go home."

"I understand you people have something to look at these days."

"What's that?"

"Zeltner's new sec'y. I understand it walks and talks."

"I haven't been over yet this week."

"Living quiff, I hear. I wish you'd check that out and tell me about it. I have to live somehow. I'm in no mood for what's out there. She goes for more tests tomorrow. Fucking doctor says it could be cancer."

"Let's have lunch sometime."

Pammy thought of the elevators in the World Trade Center as "places." She asked herself, not without morbid scorn: "When does this place get to the forty-fourth floor?" Or: "Isn't it just a matter of time before this place gets stuck with me inside it?" Elevators were supposed to be enclosures. These were too big, really, to fit that description. These also had

different doors for entering and leaving, certainly a distinguishing feature of places more than of elevators.

If the elevators were places, the lobbies were "spaces." She
felt abstract terms were called for in the face of such tyrannic
grandeur. Four times a day she was dwarfed, progressively
midgeted, walking across that purplish-blue rug. Spaces. In-
definite locations. Positions regarded as occupied by something.

From Grief's offices she looked across the landfill, the piers,
the western extremities of anonymous streets. Even at this
height she could detect the sweltering intensity, a slow roiling
force. It moved up into the air, souls of the living.

2

Lyle shaved symmetrically, doing one segment on the left side
of his face, then the corresponding segment on the right. After
each left-right series, the lather that remained was evenly dis-
tributed.

Crossing streets in the morning, Pammy was wary of cars
slipping out from behind her and suddenly bulking into view,
forcing her to stop as they made their turns. The city functioned on principles of intimidation. She knew this and tried to
be ready, unafraid to stride across the angling path of a fender
that probed through heavy pedestrian traffic.

The car turning into Liberty Street didn't crowd her at all.
But unexpectedly it slowed as she began to cross. The driver

had one hand on the wheel, his left, and sat with much of his back resting against the door. He was virtually facing her and she was moving directly toward him. She saw through the window that his legs were well apart, left foot apparently on the brake. His right hand was at his crotch, rubbing. She was vaguely aware of two or three other people crossing the street. The driver looked directly at her, then glanced at his hand. His look was businesslike, a trifle hurried. She turned away and walked down the middle of the street, intending to cross well beyond the rear of the car. The man accelerated, heading east toward Broadway.

They roamed in cars now. This was new to her. She felt acute humiliation, a sure knowledge of having been reduced in worth. She walked a direct line toward the north tower but had no real sense of destination. Her anger was imparted to everything around her. She moved through enormous smudges, fields of indistinct things. In a sense there was no way to turn down that kind of offer. To see the offer made was to accept, automatically. He'd taken her into his car and driven to some freight terminal across the river, where he'd parked near an outbuilding with broken windows. There he'd taught her his way of speaking, his beliefs and customs, the names of his mother and father. Having done this, he no longer needed to put hands upon her. They were part of each other now. She carried him around like a dead beetle in her purse.

In college the girls in her dormitory wing had referred to perverts as "verts." They reacted to noises in the woods beyond their rooms by calling along the hall: "Vert alert, vert alert." Pammy turned into the entrance and walked across the huge lobby now, the north space, joined suddenly by thousands coming from other openings, mainly from the subway concourses where gypsy vendors sold umbrellas from nooks in the unfinished construction. They'd been stupid to make a rhyme of it.

Lyle checked his pockets for change, keys, wallet, cigarettes, pen and memo pad. He did this six or seven times a day, absently, his hand merely skimming over trousers and jacket, while he was walking, after lunch, leaving cabs. It was a routine that required no conscious planning yet reassured him, and this was supremely important, of the presence of his objects and their locations. He stacked coins on the dresser at home. Sometimes he tried to see how long he could use a face towel before its condition forced him to put it in the hamper. Often he wore one of the three or four neckties whose design and color he didn't really like. Other ties he used sparingly, the good ones, preferring to see them hanging in the closet. He drew pleasure from the knowledge that they'd outlast the inferior ties.

He was sandy-haired and tall, his firm's youngest partner. Although he'd never worn glasses, someone or other was always asking what had happened to them. A quality of self-possession, maybe, of near-effeteness, implied the suitability of glasses. Some of the same people, and others, watching him shake a cigarette out of the pack, asked him when he'd started smoking. Lyle was secretly hurt by these defects of focus or memory on the part of acquaintances. The real deficiency, somehow, he took to be his.

There was a formality about his movements, a tiller-distinct precision. He rarely seemed to hurry, even on the trading floor, but this was deceptive, a result of steady pace, the drift-less way he maneuvered through a room. His body was devoid of excess. He had no chest hair, nothing but downy growth on his arms and legs. His eyes were grayish and mild, conjuring distances. This pale stare, the spareness of his face, its lack of stark lines, the spaces in his manner made people feel he would be hard to know.

The old man was outside Federal Hall again, leaky-eyed and grizzled, holding his sign up over his head—the banks, the tanks, the corporations. The sign had narrow wooden slats fastened to each vertical border, making it relatively steady in the breeze, when there was a breeze. Lyle crossed diagonally toward the Exchange. The air was smothering already. By the close of trading, people would be looking for places to hide. In the financial district everything tended to edge beyond ac-ceptability. The tight high buildings held things in, cross-reflecting heat, channeling oceanic gusts all winter long. It was a test environment for extreme states of mind as well. Every day the outcasts were in the streets, women with junk carts, a man dragging a mattress, ordinary drunks slipping in from the dock areas, from construction craters near the Hudson, people without shoes, amputees and freaks, men splitting off from groups sleeping in fish crates under the highway and limping down past the slips and lanes, the helicopter pad, onto Broad Street, living rags. Lyle thought of these people as infiltrators in the district. Elements filtering in. Nameless arrays of exis-tence. The use of madness and squalor as texts in the denun-ciation of capitalism did not strike him as fitting here, despite appearances. It was something else these men and women had

come to mean, shouting, trailing vomit on their feet. The sign-
holder outside Federal Hall was not part of this. He was in
context here, professing clearly his opposition.

Lyle made small talk with the others at his booth. The chart
for a baseball pool was taped to the wall above a telephone.
The floor began to fill. People generally were cheerful. There
was sanity here, even at the wildest times. It was all worked
out. There were rules, standards and customs. In the electronic clatter it was possible to feel you were part of a breath-
takingly intricate quest for order and elucidation, for identity
among the constituents of a system. Everyone reconnoitered
toward a balance. After the cries of the floor brokers, the
quotes, the bids, the cadence and peal of an auction market,
there was always a final price, good or bad, a leveling out of
the world's creaturely desires. Floor members were down-
to-earth. They played practical jokes. They didn't drift beyond the margins of things. Lyle wondered how much of
the world, the place they shared a lucid view of, was still his
to live in.

Moments before noon something happened near post 12.
To Lyle it seemed at first an indistinct warp, a collapse in
pattern. He perceived a rush, unusual turbulence, people
crowding and looking around. He realized the sharp noise
he'd heard seconds earlier was gunfire. He thought: *small
arms*. There was another burst of activity, this one more
ragged, at post 4, nearer Lyle, not far from the entrance to the
blue room annex. People were shouting, a few individuals,
uncertainly, their voices caught in a hail of polite surprise. He
saw the first clear action, men moving quickly through the
crowd, sideways, skipping between people, trying to hand-

force a path. They were chasing someone. He approached the
entrance to the blue room. Total confusion in there. A guard
brushed by him. It was not possible to run in this gathering.
Everyone moving quickly went sideways or three-quarters, in
little hop-steps. The electronic gong sounded. At the far end of
the room he saw heads bobbing above the crowd, a line of
them, the chasers. The people in the blue room didn't know
where to look. A young woman, a messenger in a blue smock,
covered her mouth with the piece of paper she'd been taking
somewhere. Lyle turned and went over to post 12. There was
a body. Someone was giving mouth-to-mouth. Blood spread
over the victim's chest. Lyle saw a man step back from a small
inching trickle on the floor. Everyone here was attentive. A
stillness had washed up. It was the calmest pocket on the floor
right now.

Later that afternoon he had a drink with Frank McKechnie
in a bar not far from the Exchange. McKechnie was beginning
to look like some crime czar's personal chauffeur. He was
stocky, grayer by the day, and his clothing could barely resist
the surge of firmness and girth that had been taking place
these past few years. They smoked quietly for a moment, looking into rows of bottles. McKechnie had ordered two cold
draft beers, stressing cold, almost belligerent about it.

"What do we know?"

"George Sedbauer."

"Doesn't sound familiar," Lyle said.

"I knew George. George was an interesting guy. He could
charm people. Charm the ass off anybody. But he had this
thing, this almost gift for complications. He would find ways
to get into trouble. If a way didn't exist, he'd invent one. He

was in trouble with the Board more than once. George was likable but you never knew where he was."

"Until now."

"You know now."

"I heard they caught up to the guy down on Bridge Street or somewhere?"

"They got him in the bond room. He never made it out to the street."

"I heard street."

"He made it no further than the bond room," McKechnie said. "Whoever told you Bridge Street, tell him he's spinning a web of lies."

"I heard he made it out."

"Sheer fantasy."

"A trail of deceit, is that it?"

"What did you hear about his identity?"

"Nothing," Lyle said.

"That's good, because there's nothing to hear. That anybody's heard of, he never existed before today. Hey, when the hell are you coming up to have dinner with us with your goddamn spouse and all?"

"We never seem to get out."

"My wife is still with the tests."

"We seem to have trouble getting out. We're not organized. She's as bad as I am. One of these days we'll get organized enough."

"You sure you're married, Lyle? There's talk you got something going with so many women in so many places, you couldn't possibly have a wife too. I hear talk."

Lyle blinked into his beer, smiling lightly.

"He had a visitor's badge, I understand."

"Correct," McKechnie said.

"Well whose visitor? Obviously that's the thing."

"He was George Sedbauer's visitor."

"I didn't know that."

"George got him on the floor."

"Well you have to wonder if they knew each other why the guy would shoot him right there instead of some side street."

"Maybe it wasn't planned, to shoot him."

"They had an argument," Lyle said.

"They had an argument and the guy whips out a handgun. Which they recovered, incidentally. A starter's pistol with the barrel bored out to take twenty-two-caliber ammunition."

"How do you have an argument with an outsider on the floor? Who on the floor has time to get into an argument with someone who's his own guest?"

"Not everybody with a guest badge is your sister-in-law from East Hartford. Maybe George had interesting friends."

With his index finger McKechnie made a wigwag motion over the glasses. The bartender moved their way, talking to someone over his shoulder.

"You know what it all means, don't you?"

"Tell me, Frank."

"It means they'll install one of those metal detection devices and we'll all have to walk through it every time we go on the floor. I hate those goddamn things. They can damage your bone marrow. My life is crud enough as it is."

3

Lyle sat by a window at home, in T-shirt and jeans, barefoot, drinking Irish lager.

Pammy bought fruit at a sidewalk stand. She loved the look of fruit in crates, outdoors, tiers of peaches and grapes. Buying fresh fruit made her feel good. It was an act of moral excellence. She looked forward to taking the grapes home, putting them in a bowl and letting cold water run over the bunches. It gave her such pleasure, hefting one of the bunches in her hand, feeling the water come cooling through. Then there were peaches. The earthly merit of peaches.

Lyle remembered having seen some pennies in the bedroom. He went in there. Ten minutes later he found them, three, sitting on a copper-and-brown Kleenex box. He heard Pam take the keys out of her purse. He stacked the pennies on the dresser. Transit tokens on the right side of the dresser. Pennies on the left. He went back to the window.

Pammy had to put down the bag of fruit before she could get the door opened. She remembered what had been bothering her, the vague presence. Her life. She hated her life. It was a minor thing, though, a small bother. She tended to forget about it. When she recalled what it was that had been on her mind, she felt satisfied at having remembered and relieved that it was nothing worse. She pushed into the apartment.

"There she is."

"Hi, you're home."

"What's in that big wet funny bag?"

"I may not show you."

"Fruit."

"I got you some cantaloupe."

"Do I like cantaloupe, he asked," Lyle said.

"And these plums, can you believe them?"

"Who'll eat all that? You never eat any. You eat a little bit when you take it out of the bag and then that's it, Chiquita. In the fruit thing to shrivel."

"You like plums."

"Then you say it's for me, look what I got you, world's greatest tangerine, glom glom."

"Well I think fruit's pretty."

"In the fruit bin to shrivel up like fetuses."

"Where's my beer?" she said.

He had a look on his face, supposedly an imitation of her virtuous-fruit look, that made her laugh. She moved through the apartment, taking off clothes, putting the fruit away, getting cheese and crackers. There were pieces of her everywhere. Lyle watched, humming something.

"A guy got killed today on the floor, shot."

"What, at the Exchange?"

"Somebody shot him, out of nowhere."

"Did you see it?"

"Ping."

"Christ, who? Puerto Ricans again?"

He reached out when she went by. She moved into him as he rose from the chair. She felt his thumb at the small of her back, slipping inside elastic. She reached behind him to draw the curtains. He sat back down, humming something, arms raised, as she lifted the T-shirt off him.

"I wouldn't want to say porta rickens. I wouldn't want to
say coloreds or any of the well-meaning white folks who have
taken up the struggle against the struggle, not knowing, you
see, that the capitalist system and the power structure and the
pattern of repression are themselves a struggle. It's not an easy
matter, being the oppressor. A lot of work involved. Hard
dogged unglamorous day-to-day toil. Pounding the pavement.
Checking records and files. Making phone call after phone
call. Successful oppression depends on this. So I would say in
conclusion that they are struggling against the struggle. But I
wouldn't want to say porta rickens, commanists, what-have-
you. It be no bomb, remember. It be a gun, ping."

Pammy and Lyle, undressed, were face to face on the white
bed, kneeling, hands on each other's shoulders, in flat light,
dimming in tenths of seconds. The room was closed off to the
street's sparse evening, the hour of thoughtful noises, when
everything is interim. The air conditioner labored, an uphill
tone. There were intermittent lights in the distance, high-
tension streaks. With each discharge a neutral tint, a residue,
as of cooled ash, penetrated the room. Pammy and Lyle began
to touch. They knew the shifting images of physical similarity.
It was an unspoken bond, part of their shared consciousness,
the mined silence between people who live together. Curling
across each other's limbs and silhouettes they seemed repeat-
able, daughter cells of some precise division. Their tongues
drifted over wetter flesh. It was this divining of moisture, an
intuition of nature submerged, that set them at each other,
nipping, in eager searches. He tasted vinegar in her spinning
hair. They parted a moment, touched from a studied distance,
testing introspectively, a complex exchange. He left the bed to

turn off the air conditioner and raise the window. Evening was recharged and fragrant. Thunder sounded right over them. The best things about summer were these storms, filling a room, almost medicinally, with weather, with variable light. Rain struck the window in pellets. They could see trees out back take the stiff winds. Lyle had gotten wet, opening the window, his hands and belly, and they waited for him to dry, talking in foreign accents about a storm they'd driven through in the Alps somewhere, laughing in "Portuguese" and "Dutch." She twisted into him, their solitude become a sheltering in this rain. They lost contact for a moment. She brought him back, needing that conflict of surfaces, the palpable logic of his cock inside her. Then she was gripping hard, released to the contagion of recurring motion, rising, as they ached and played, sunny as young tigers.

It is time to "perform," he thought. She would have to be "satisfied." He would have to "service" her. They would make efforts to "interact."

When he was sure they were finished he moved away, feeling the barest spray of rain after it hit the window ledge. On their backs they reorganized their breathing. She wanted pizza. It made her feel guilty not to want fruit. But she'd worked all day, taken elevators and trains. She couldn't deal with the consequences of fruit, its perishability, the duty involved in eating it. She wanted to sit in a corner, alone, and stuff herself with junk.

She is padding to the bathroom, he thought.

It grew darker. She sat at the foot of the bed, dressing. The rain slackened. She heard the Mister Softee truck down in the street. It announced itself with recorded music, a sound she hated, the same cranked-out mechanical whine every night. She couldn't hear that noise without feeling severe mental oppression. To indicate this, she made a low droning sound, the tremulous *m* that meant she was on the edge of something.

"There really is a Mister Softee."

"I believe," she said.

"He sits in the back of the truck. That's him making the noise. It's not music on a record or tape. That's his mouth. It's coming out of his mouth. That's his language. They speak that way in the back of ice cream trucks all over the city. I won't say nation yet. It hasn't spread."

"A local phenomenon."

"He sits back there dribbling. He's very fat and pastelike. He can't get up. His flesh doesn't have the right consistency."

"He has no genitals."

"They're in there somewhere."

"Kidding aside, let's talk," she said.

She crawled along the bed, wearing a shirt and jeans, and settled next to him, pressing contentedly. He made a sound, then started to bite her head. She scratched lightly at his ribs.

"Better watch."

"I bite heads for a living."

"Better watch, you. I know where and how to strike."

He made gulping sounds. This seemed to interest him more than most noises he made. He evolved chokes and gasps out of the original sound. He began to drown or suffocate, making convulsive attempts to breathe. Pammy answered the phone on the fourth or fifth ring, as she always did, either, he thought, because she considered it chic, or just to annoy him. It was

Ethan Segal. He and Jack were dropping over. What do we have to drink?

Lyle called Dial-a-Steak. By the time the food arrived, everyone was a little drunk. Ethan shuffled to the table, a chess-playing smile on his face. They sat down, having brought their drinks with them, and began to strip aluminum foil from the steak, the salad, the potatoes, the bread, the salt and pepper.

"It's Jack's birthday."

No one said anything.

"I'm thirty."

"Welcome to Death Valley," Lyle said.

"I feel different."

"But none the wiser," Ethan said.

"I used to think thirty was so old. I'd meet people who were thirty and I'd think God, thirty."

"Wait till you're fortyish," Ethan said. "All hell breaks loose for about ten minutes. Then you begin to grow old quietly. It's not bad, really. You begin wearing house slippers to the theater and people think you're some unbelievably interesting man about to get written up in What's Happening, you know, or People Are Talking About, in *Vogue* or some such."

"We forgot to open the wine," Jack said.

"At what specific time," Pammy said, "does one become fortyish?"

"Wine, Lyle."

"We're out. There is no wine. Our cellar was auctioned off to pay taxes on the estate."

"We brought wine," Jack said. "We came with wine."

"There is no wine, Jack. You're free to look around."

"It's in the cab," Ethan said.

Jack said: "The cab."

"We left it in the cab. I remember distinctly that we had it when we got in the cab and I don't recall seeing it after that."

"Because you drank it," Pammy said.

"Because I drank the wine in the cab."

"Do I hear diet cola?" Jack said.

They were talking quickly and getting laughs on intonation alone, the prospect of wit. This isn't really funny, Lyle thought. It seems funny because we're getting half smashed. But nobody's really saying funny things. Tomorrow she'll say what a funny night and I'll say it just seemed funny and she'll give me a look. She'll give me a look—he saw the look but did not express it in verbal form, going on to the next space-less array, a semi-coherent framework of atomic "words." But I'll know I'm right because I'm making this mental note right now to remind myself tomorrow that we're not really being funny.

Shut up, he told himself.

Jack Laws nurtured an element of hysteria in his laugh. His head went tilt, his hands came up to his chest in paw form and he shook out some cries of phobic joy. It was an up-to-date cultural mannerism, an index of the suspicion that nothing we say or do can be properly gauged without reference to the fear that pervades every situation and specific thing. Jack was broad-shouldered and short. He had a snub nose, small mouth and well-cleft chin. His face, over all, possessed a sly innocence that quickly shaded off into grades of uncertainty or combativeness, depending on the situation. His presence in a room was an asset at most gatherings. The area he occupied seemed a pocket of sociability and cheer. In some rooms, however, people's reactions to Jack, whether friendly or indifferent, were based on their feelings for Ethan. Pammy was aware of these angles of reflection. She tried to divert Jack at such times, subtly.

Ethan was back in the armchair, smiling cryptically again. He was onto vodka, neat. Jack finished off Pammy's steak, talking at the same time about a friend of his who was in training to swim some strait in Europe, the first ever to attempt it north to south, or something. There was a comedy record on the stereo. It was Lyle's latest. He played such records often, getting the routines down pat, the phrasing, the dialects, then repeating the whole thing for people on the floor in slack times. This one he played for Ethan's benefit. He watched Ethan, studying his reaction, as the record played, as Jack ate and talked, as Pammy wandered around the room. After a while he followed her over to the bookshelves.

"Did you pay the Saks thing?"

"No, what thing?"

"They're panting," he said. "They're enclosing slips with the bill. Little reminders. They're calling you Ms."

"Next week."

"You said that."

"They'll wait."

"Where did I tell you the battery was for the Italian clock when the one in there now runs out?"

"I don't know."

"You forgot already."

"What battery?" she said.

"I went to nine places, looking. It's one point four volts.

You can't go around the corner. It's a certain size. Least you
could do is remember where it is when I tell you."

"There's a battery *in* there."

"For when it runs out," he said. "It's a ten-month-some-odd
life expectancy and we've had the clock nearly that long already."

"Okay, where's the battery?"

"In the kitchen drawer with the corkscrews and ribbons."

Lyle went into the bedroom and turned on the TV set. That
was the only light. He watched for a few minutes, then began
coasting along the dial. Jack came in and he had to stop. It
made Lyle nervous to watch television with someone in the
room, even Pammy, even when he wasn't changing channels
every twenty seconds. There was something private about
television. It was intimate, able to cause embarrassment.

"What's on?"

"Not much."

"You watch a lot?" Jack said. "I do."

"Sometimes."

"It keeps the mind off things. You don't have to involve
yourself too much. Listen, talk, anything."

"I talk all day," Lyle said.

"Exactly, I know."

Jack hadn't moved from the doorway. He was eating a
peach, standing in light from the hall. When he turned and
laughed, reacting to something Ethan or Pam had said, Lyle
saw the patch of white hair above his neck. He thought of
saying something about it but by the time Jack turned his head
again, he'd lost interest.

"Bed's a mess but come on in, find a chair, cetra cetra."

"That's okay, I'm just snooping around."

"Nothing's on, looks like."

"But can you believe what they show sometimes? I think it's disgusting, Lyle. I can't believe. It's so sleazy. Who are those people? I refuse to watch. I totally do not watch. Ethan watches."

"Sometimes you see something, you know, interesting in another sense. I don't know."

"What other sense?"

"I don't know."

"I totally cannot believe. What goes on. Right there on TV."

"What are you doing these days, Jack?"

"I'm thinking of getting a scheme together."

"What kind?"

"I know where I can get microfilmed mailing lists of two hundred thousand subscribers to these eight or nine health publications. I think it's A to M."

"You'll, what, sell them?"

"Sell them."

"What else, of course."

"Sell them, what else?"

They watched and listened for ten minutes as two announcers tried to fill time during a rain delay at a ball game.

"We have two sets," Jack said.

"I'm thinking of that."

"I made him get an extra."

He laughed lightly, ending on a note of apprehension, and went back inside. Pammy was sitting on the floor. With her index finger she kept tapping an ice cube in her glass, watching it plunge briefly, then surge.

"You know what I don't think?" she said. "I don't think I can stand the idea of tomorrow."

She looked at Ethan, who stared into the carpet.

"I really, it seems, I don't think."

"It's that time of night," Jack said.

"It's just that I can't accommodate any more time than what's right here. It's, where we go, your friend here, together with me. Choose precisely the word, for this is important. Not place, which is the elevator's word. Not office or building, which are too common and apply anywhere."

"Environment."

"Thank you, Jack."

"Should I make coffee?"

"No, no, this isn't a coffee conversation. This is a gut topic. Wait a minute now, I'll get to it. Don't think I don't know that your friend here has not in the longest time made the slightest remark to his job. Why? Because you know as well as I do, Jack, what happens to people. Your friend here used to joke. You recall it, Jack, as well as I do. We both heard this man. He'd be so funny about his job and those people in the field. The stories. Do you believe? Per diem rates for terminal-illness counseling? So if it drags on, forget it, we got you by the balls? And the woman in Syracuse? With the grief-stricken pet, what was it, canary, in Syracuse, that the other one died —not canary, what, shit, I'm screwing this up. But that's okay. You're dear friends. We're dear friends here. But he no longer does it. That's the point and he thinks I don't notice. Because it's so stupid. It's so modern-stupid. It's this thing that people are robots that scares me. And the environment, Jack, thank you."

"I never heard about the grief-stricken canary."

"Jack, you heard. We all did." She pointed toward the bedroom. "He still talks about it. Just say Syracuse to Lyle, blink-blink-blink, the way he laughs, right, with the eyelids."

Ethan made a sweeping movement with his arm, a gesture of cancellation. His cravat, an ironic adornment to begin with, had slipped over the front of his shirt so that he appeared to be wearing a child's scarf.

"The thing is," he said.

They waited.

"To forge a change that you may be reluctant to forge, that may be problematical for this or that reason, you have to tell people. You have to talk and tell people. Jack sees what I'm getting at. You have to bring it out. Even if you have no intention at the time of doing it out of whatever fear or trembling, you still must make it begin to come true by articulating it. This changes the path of your life. Just telling people makes the change begin to happen. If, in the end, you choose to keep going with whatever you've been doing that's been this problematical thing in your life, well and good, it's up to you. But if you need to feel you're on the verge of a wonderful change, whether you are or not, the thing to do is tell people. 'I am on the verge of a wonderful change. I am about to do something electrifying. The very fibers of your being will be electrified, sir, when I tell you what it is I propose to do.' To speak it in words is to see the possibility emerge. Doesn't matter what. Don't bother your head over what. For the purposes of this discussion it could be mountain-climbing we're talking about or this friend of Jack, the oft-mentioned scaly chap who plans to swim the North Sea left-handed. Our lives are enriched by these little blurbs we send each other. These things are necessary to do. 'I am going back to school to learn Arabic, whatever.' Say it to people for six months. 'I am going to live in Maine or else.' Jack sees my point. Tell people, tell them. Make something up. The important thing is to seem to be on the verge. Then it begins to come true, a little bit. I don't know, maybe talking is enough. Maybe you don't want to forge the change. Maybe telling people *is* the change. How should I know? Why ask me? Lyle, where is Lyle? Say good night to Lyle."

"I think I know what you mean," Pammy said.

"Do you see a glimmer?"

"I think I see a glimmer."

"We'll hail a cab, Jack. Our bottle of wine will be in the back seat. It will complete the circle. I believe in circles."

"Jack, really, happy birthday, I mean it."

"I tried to get drunk."

"Needn't apologize," she said. "Tell your friend here I think I see what he means."

"Well I don't," Jack said.

In the bedroom Lyle watched television. Pammy came in, sat at the end of the bed, where earlier she'd dressed, and undressed. It made little or no sense, all this undressing, dressing. If you calculated the time. Hours spent. After a while she stood up, nude, and walked to Lyle, who sat in a director's chair, his back to her. She put her hands on his shoulders. The volume on the TV set was turned way down. She heard cars outside, the sound of tires on a wet street, whispered *s*'s. Her face had Nordic contours and looked flawless in this light. He extended one arm across his chest and gripped her hand in his.

4

After the close Lyle walked north on Pearl. Currents of humid air swept through the streets. As he waited for a light to change he became aware of a figure nearby, a furtive woman, literally inching toward him. He turned slightly, nearly facing her. She stopped then and spoke, although not directly to Lyle, her head averted somewhat.

"She's a man's toilet, a whore. He's legally disabled meanwhile. He sits with his clocks and watches, knowing she's out of his sight, being a toilet for men. Three in the morning. Four in the morning. Please, who needs it? For him, special, she'll drop dead. I'm expecting it shortly."

Lyle noted that she was in her fifties, stunted somewhat, normally dressed, probably not Jewish despite the faint lilt to her voice. He went east on John Street, enumerating these facts as though he were conversing with someone who sought a description of the woman. This was something he did only on buses as a rule. His attention would wander to someone across the aisle and he'd find himself putting together a physical description of the man or woman—almost always a man. The notion of police interrogation was part of the mental concept. He was a witness identifying a suspect. These interludes

developed without planning; he simply found himself relating
(to someone) the color of a particular man's shoes, trousers
and jacket, his estimated height and weight, black man, white
man, so forth. When he realized he was doing it, he stopped,
telling himself to shut up. Sometimes, walking, he memorized
the numbers on license plates of certain cars. Hours later he'd
repeat the number to make sure he still knew it. The testing of
a perennial witness.

Near the foot of John Street was the toy skyscraper where
his firm had offices. The benches outside were painted in pri-
mary colors, as were various decorations on the lower façade.
He thought of building blocks and games with flashing lights.
There were whimsical phone booths and a superdigital clock.
To get to the elevator bank he went through a blue neon
tunnel. He got off the elevator and was stopped by Teddy
Mackel, a middle-aged man in charge of the mail room.

"I think you ought to walk by Zeltner's room, Lyle."

"I heard."

"Makes me want to take back my chastity vow that I took
when I was with the Marist Brothers earlier in this century,
Lyle, Jesus."

"We need it around here, something, for morale"

"Tall, I like that about a woman. Tall, nice."

"More there."

"Never end a sentence with a preposition," Mackel said.
"That's the other thing I learned when I was with the Marists.
They're a teaching order. Those were the two things they
taught us. Chastity and how to end sentences. Which one did
me less good I bet you can guess."

"Neck to neck, I judge it."

"Tell me confidentially, will we survive, Lyle? My kids are worried. They want to finish college. You're down there in the dust of battle. Say some words to our viewing audience."

There was an alcove outside Zeltner's office. She was at the desk there, reading a paperback book, her shoulders hunched in a way that indicated a special depth of solitude, he thought, like a figure in a Hopper painting. He came back the other way now, having stopped at the water cooler. Fairly long blond hair. That was about all that registered. He stopped at the end of the hall, wondering what to do next. There were two or three people he could visit, more or less plausibly, in their offices. He didn't feel like doing that but didn't want to leave either. Leaving presented a void. He heard the elevator door open and decided he couldn't stand around any longer. He went back to the alcove. He leaned over, tapping his index finger on the surface of the desk.

"Where is he? Is he around somewhere?"

"He didn't say."

"Nothing's moving in there."

"I don't know where he is."

"The elusive Zeltner."

"He forgets to tell me."

"That's right, I forgot that about him."

"Who should I say was asking?"

"Not important, really, I'll come back."

Blond hair, little or no makeup, blank sort of face with nice enough features. Teeth and nails on the drab side. Blondness and probably great figure would account for local acclaim. Must be seen in motion no doubt.

Pammy on the eighty-third floor of the north tower contrived to pass the time by devising a question for Ethan Segal. If the elevators in the World Trade Center were places, as she believed them to be, and if the lobbies were spaces, as she further believed, what then was the World Trade Center itself? Was it a condition, an occurrence, a physical event, an existing circumstance, a presence, a state, a set of invariables? Ethan didn't respond and she changed the subject, watching him type figures into little boxes on a long form, folded over his machine, crowding down on it, only his fingers moving.

"We have nothing planned," she said. "Lyle doesn't think he'll be able to get away. It's very hair-raising right now, I gather. He's talking about not before October."

"That's a nice time, really."

"I think it would be specially nice if we did something together."

"Where?"

"Wherever."

"Vales of time and space."

"I think it would work very well, Ethan. It can be wearing, just two. We all get along."

"Lyle's not available, so."

"You wouldn't consider October as soon enough, I don't imagine."

"I'd never last it out, Pam."

"This city."

"July, August."

"I'm thinking about tap-dancing lessons," she said.

"Let me type."

"No comment?"

"Let me type awhile," he said. "I like filling these little

boxes with numbers. Numbers are indispensable to my world view at present. I don't believe I'm doing this. This is some toad's chore. But I genuinely enjoy it. It's so anally satisfying. Contentment at last."

Late one afternoon Lyle waited outside the building on John Street. When she came out, in a crowd, he realized it would be awkward, physically and otherwise, to try to isolate her from the others. She might not recognize him. Someone from the office might see them and come over to join the conversation. He followed her half a block, not yet trying to catch up. At the corner she got into a waiting car, which moved off quickly. He felt resentful, as if he'd been supplanted by another man. It was a green VW, California plates 180 BOA.

He sat on a bench in a plaza overlooking the river. He felt lessened somehow. Freighter cranes slanted across the tops of sheds in the Brooklyn dock area. It was the city, the heat, an endless sense of repetition. The district repeated itself in blocks of monochromatic stone. He was present in *things*. There was more of him here through the idle nights than he took home with him to vent and liberate. He thought about the nights. He imagined the district never visited, empty of human transaction, and how buildings such as these would seem to hold untouchable matter, enormous codifications of organic decay. He tried to examine the immense complexity of going home.

The next afternoon he managed to reach her before she joined the flow into the streets. He spoke through a reassuring smile. He concentrated on this expression to the degree that he could visualize his own lips moving. It was a moment of utter disengagement. He didn't know what he was saying and with people swarming around them and traffic building nearby he could barely hear her voice when she replied, as she did once or twice, briefly, in phrases as translucent as his own. He guided her unobtrusively toward a quieter part of the arcade, trying to reconstruct the first stages of their conversation even as he continued to babble and gleam. He wasn't yet certain she recognized him.

"The floor," he said.

Her reply made no sense. It went right through him, suffused with light. He leaned closer and renewed his smile, warmly. This would keep him from blinking. He blinked only with tight smiles, for emphasis.

"The Exchange," he said. "You've seen me outside Zeltner's office. I know, people you've seen just once, hard to place, I realize. Is there the subway? I'll walk along. Where do you live? Queens, I'll wager. I like it out there, despite people saying Queens, what, where, my God. It's metaphysical."

"I usually get a ride."

"I understand there's a certain insecurity in the Zeltner power alley. You've been up there how long now? Let's stand over in the shade. Queens is endless. This endless something about it. It's like a maze without the interconnections. A bland maze. I have a theory about where people live in New York."

She wore a white blouse, pleated blue skirt and white shoes. As he talked and then listened he tested himself by recalling the VW's license number. It completed a mental set. They walked slowly to the corner where she'd been picked up the day before.

"This is where my ride should come."

"Is it all right if I wait?"

"I guess."

"What's your name?"

"Rosemary Moore."

"I have to be up there tomorrow after the close. Maybe I'll stop by if you're not busy. We can stop off after you're through. Would that be all right? A drink or two. A quick drink as they say. Tiny. A tiny drink. They serve only tiny drinks."

This time she got into the back seat. A man and woman were in front, both somewhat older than she was, Rosemary Moore in navy and white.

5

Pammy examined the uses of boredom. Of late she'd found herself professing to be bored fairly often. She knew it was a shield for deeper feelings. Not wishing to express conventional outrage she said again and again, "How boring, so boring, I'm bored." Pornography bored her. Talk of violence made her sigh. Things in the street, just things she saw and heard day to day, forced her into subtle evasions. Her body would automatically relax. To feel this slackening take place was to complete another weary detour.

People talked to her on the bus, strangers, a little detached in tone, a little *universal,* sometimes giving the impression they were communicating *out* to her from some unbounded secret place.

Flying made her yawn. She yawned on the elevators at the World Trade Center. Often she yawned in banks, waiting on line to reach the teller. Banks made her guilty. Tellers and bank officers were always asking her to sign forms, or to re-sign forms already bearing her signature, or to provide further identification. It was her own money she wanted to draw out, obviously, but there was still this bubble of nervousness and guilt, there was still this profound anxiety over her name, her handwriting, there was still this feeling that the core content of her personality was about to be revealed, and she would stand on line with two dozen others, roped in, yawning decorously, a suspect.

Pammy heard Lyle in the corridor outside. She leaned forward and closed the toilet door. He entered the apartment, walked down the hall, stopped outside the door, then opened it. She made a monkey face and uttered a series of panicky squeals, bouncing on the seat. He closed the door and went into the bedroom.

She called out: "What'd you get me for Valentine's Day?"

"A vasectomy," he said. "Is this February?"

"I only wish."

"Why?"

"So our vacation would be over."

"Why?"

"Because I know we're not going to take one."

"You go."

"What will you do?"

"Work," he said.

She came out of the bathroom. He followed her into the kitchen zipping up lightweight cords, his pelvis drawn back to avoid the primal snare. They jostled each other before the open refrigerator.

"Goody, cheddar."

"What's these?"

"Brandy snaps."

"Triffic."

"Look out."

"No you push me, you."

They went into the living room, each with something to eat and drink. Lyle turned on the new television set and they watched the evening news. Pammy became embarrassed on behalf of someone being interviewed, a man with a minor speech defect. She put her hands over her ears and looked away. The air conditioner made loud noises and Lyle turned it off. Then he went into the bedroom and watched television in there for a while.

"Are you watching this?" she called out.

"What, no."

"The beauty technician."

"No."

"Put it on quick."

"Gaw damn, Miss Molly, a man can't watch but one thing at a time."

"Put it on, on seven."

"Later, I'm watching."

"Now," she said. "Hurry. Hurry up. Quick, seven, you dumb."

Embodied in objects was a partial sense of sharing. They didn't lift their eyes from their respective sets. But noises bound them, a cyclist kick-starting, the plane that came winding down the five miles from its transatlantic apex, rippling the pictures on their screens. Objects were memory inert. Desk, the bed, et cetera. Objects would survive the one who died first and remind the other of how easily halved a life can become. Death, perhaps, was not the point so much as separation. Chairs, tables, dressers, envelopes. Everything was a common experience, binding them despite their indirections, the slanted apparatus of their agreeing. That they did agree was not in doubt. Faithlessness and desire. It wasn't necessary to tell them apart. His body, hers. Sex, love, monotony, contempt. The spell that had to be entered was out there among the unmemorized faces and uniform cubes of being. This, their sweet and mercenary space, was self-enchantment, the near common dream they'd countenanced for years. Only absences were fully shared.

"What's with Grief?" he called. "I don't hear lately."

"Ethan and I made a secret pact. It don't exist far's we's concerned."

"You bottomed out in the second quarter. You're in the midst of a mini-surge right now. You're also talking about diversification."

"Let me lower this."

"What?"

"Can't hear you."

"Diversification."

"Is that, what, Dow Jones or the other guys?"

"Theme attractions," he said. "That's very much a part of the shed-ule, pending word from the data retrieval chaps."

"I don't think."

"A fantasy ranch in Santa Mesa County, Arizona. Grief fantasies. People dressing up to grieve."

"Hee hee, I know you're stupid."

"No tengo tiene."

"We never eat paella," she said. "Remember the place on Charles, was it? Or West Fourth?"

"Maybe the corner," he said. "Is there a corner there?"

Her father had made her yawn. Whenever she picked up the phone to call him, she would feel her mouth gaping open with "fatigue," "boredom," her countermeasures to compelling emotion. He'd lived then near the northern point of Manhattan, mentally distressed, a man who preferred gestures to speech. During her visits he would answer most of her questions with his hands, indicating that this was all right, that was not so bad, the other was a problem. He nodded, smiled, showed her the contents of various cigar boxes and shopping bags. On the phone he begged for documents. Birth certificate, savings passbook, social security card, memberships, compensations, group plans. She'd remind him where everything was, having learned to steady her desperation until it became a stretch-tight level of patience. Sometime before he died she learned from one of his neighbors that he often stood on corners and asked people to help him cross the street, although he wasn't physically impaired. He would take the person's arm and walk to the other side, then continue slowly on his own to the next corner, where he'd wait for someone else. She wished she hadn't known that. It suggested a failure on her part, some defect of love or involvement. Dialing his number she would yawn, reflexively. Whatever the point source of this mechanical tremor, she'd learned to accept it as part of growing up and down in the vast world of other people's pain.

"There's green," she said.

Lyle sat reading alongside the set she was looking at. She faced both him and it. The book he read was hers, a history of the dance. She glanced that way every time he turned a page.

"Well dial the thing."

"Color very lurid."

"Thanks, seeing what I spent."

"Color is roloc."

"We have to connect it," he said. "It has to get hooked up on the roof."

"Roof is foor."

"They'll get a guy."

"There wis green. There wis pink. There wis o-range."

"Master antenna, as in 'master antenna.'"

Pammy sat back. She raised and flexed her legs, alternately, as though limbering up. She put her hands on her head and moved her legs faster now, cycling. After a while she stood up, took off her jeans and did stretching exercises. Lyle developed an erection. She sat and watched television. It was nearly dark. The Mister Softee truck was on their street.

"Pant, pant."

"Out of shape."

"Way out of shape," she said. "You wouldn't believe what's inside this body. What a little old dried-up crone. It's down there, hear it? Bang crash, you son of a bitch. I'd like to call someone. Run over a dog, truck, and get shot by its owner, oompty boom."

"Right, complain."

"Sympathize or you can't read my book that I purchased."

"I'm saying complain. Call Broadway Maintenance. They'll come with a light bulb next Tuesday."

She turned her attention to something in the carpet, leaning over to pick at tufts of fabric.

"Look at me when you speak. Take your face out of my purchase that I bought. We need shampoo for this rug-o and still that wax for in there which is your appointed task that you have to get."

"You'll forget. You'll go out and buy fruit."

"Your task, you."

"That's all you'll buy."

"You buy."

"You'll come home with fruit by the gross weight and announce it grandly and wash it with songs of ritual washing and put it away in the box below and it shrivels and rots every time."

"It's called a fucking crisper," she said.

"It's a bin, what kind of crisper. It's a fruit compartment."

"It's a fucking crisper, you asshole."

"Watch the tube."

"They're green, look."

"Dial the fucking dial."

"Neerg," she said. "They're all neerg. These people here are neerg."

They chattered and made sounds a while longer and got up and walked and stretched and ate-and-drank a little and bumped each other and gestured, this the commonplace aimlessness of their evenings, a retreat from stress lines and language. Pammy watched Lyle reseat himself near the TV set.

On the screen some people on a talk show discussed taxes. Something about the conversation embarrassed her. She didn't know what it was exactly. Nobody said stupid things or had speech defects. There were no public service commercials showing athletes teaching retarded children to play basketball. It wasn't a case of some woman in a news film speaking ungrammatically about her three children, just killed in a fire. (She wondered if she'd become too complex to put death before grammar.) These people discussed taxes, embarrassingly. What was happening in that little panel of light that caused her to feel such disquiet and shame? She put her hands over her ears and watched Lyle read.

Early the next morning he was with Rosemary Moore in a place with exposed beams, fake, Oscar's Lounge, and a coat of arms of some sort over the bar, sitting at a table in a dark corner, solemnly watching the other patrons. A waiter kept moving in and out of the swinging doors that led to the kitchen, talking angrily as he emerged, beginning to grouse again even before he'd re-entered. For a while they listened to his argument with the unseen chef.

"This is the kind of place," Lyle said, "where the ketchup always comes out of the bottle without having to hit the bottom. Don't ask me what that means but it's true. I like this kind of eerie sameness about this kind of place. It's metaphysical."

"My drink is way too strong."

"I'll get another."

"It's all right."

"No problem, I'll get another."

"No, it's all right."

"It's all right, *Lyle*," he said. "We're using names today."

Everything he said and did seemed all right to her. It was all right to come for a drink so long as she didn't stay too long. The walk over here was all right. The place itself was all right. It was all right to sit either at the bar or back here. Again there was a lull as they watched the other customers. Everybody seemed to be having a better time than they were. It was hard to tell whether Rosemary was uncomfortable. There were shades of blandness from genial to serene; hers was closer to the median, lacking distinctive character, dead on.

"So you've been with the firm how long?"

"About three weeks now."

"Before this, what?"

"I had a job where I was on the phone all day talking to buyers. That was crazy. Then I was a stewardess, which was all right at first, places to see. Then a friend got me a job in a shipping office. That wasn't too bad but I got mononucleosis. I was a temp for a while after that. Then I got this."

"We hope you'll stay."

"I have to see."

"Do you smoke, Rosemary? See, I'm using names. Mustn't forget that."

"Some people can never quit. I smoke for a few days and then I stop. Getting addicted to things is in your personality. Somehow I can stop."

"Where do you live?"

"Queens."

"Of course."

"You should see the rents, what difference."

"My powers grow stronger with age."

"But you have to get there," she said.

"What about when you were a stewardess? You were right there. You lived in a high rise with four hundred other girls in their neatsy-clean uniforms. Always near the phone. Sorry, love, I'm on standby. Roach coach to San Juan."

"I'm lucky I have friends with a car," she said. "Except the traffic."

"Can't trust those porta rickens to sit there like civilized folks. I don't mind the cha-cha music but when they start in with the green bananas, it's too much, the FAA ought to do something, banana peels coming out of the overhead compartments not to mention in the seat things inside that wrinkled cloth. You know that wrinkled cloth?"

He caught the waiter's eye and gestured. The man brought two more drinks. Lyle felt a strange desolation pass over him. They sat awhile in silence. He watched a man at the bar put a partially melted ice cube in his mouth.

"This is my last," Rosemary said.

"If it's too strong, I'll get him to take it back."

"I don't think it will be."

"Cigarette?"

"I just finished but all right."

"How did you get your job, this one, if I can ask?"

"This girl I used to know's brother."

"She was with the firm, or he was, I guess."

"He used to be in the stock market but not our company."

"Maybe I know him."

"I don't know," she said.

"What's his name?"

"George Sedbauer."

"You see me pause," he said. "That's the guy got shot."

"I know."

"His sister was a friend of yours and you met George through her and then he more or less recommended you or gave your name to someone."

"He told me who to see and all."

"Did you know him well? I didn't know him at all but a friend of mine knew him and we talked about it after it happened, Frank McKechnie, in this bar right there."

"I met him at a party type thing. We were introduced. His sister Janet. He was very nice. I used to laugh."

"How long ago was this?"

"Two years? I don't know."

"But you had time to get to know him fairly well."

"I liked his macabre humor," she said. "George could be very macabre."

Briefly he envied Sedbauer, dead or not. He always envied men who'd done something to impress a woman. He didn't like hearing women mention another man favorably, even if he didn't know the man, or if the man was disfigured, living in the Amazon Basin, or dead. She turned her head to exhale. The waiter came out of the kitchen, talking.

"What about something to eat? I'd like to hear more. We can go somewhere decent. I just thought this place was convenient and not the big cocktail hour with huge swarms."

"I can't stay."

"Another drink then."

"This one's full."

"I'd like to hear more, really."

"About what?"

"You, I guess. I think it's interesting you knew Sedbauer. I was a few yards from the body when I guess he died. The man who did it was George's guest that day. Did you know that?"

"Yes."

"I think it's interesting. I wonder what happened between them. George was in trouble with the Board, you know. Did you know that? The Exchange Board of Directors. George was apparently a little this way and that. Not quite your run-of-the-mill dues-paying member. I wonder what he was doing with this guy wearing a guest badge and carrying a gun. We go through all those days not questioning. It's all so organized. Even the noise is organized. I'd like to question a little bit, to ask what this is, what that is, where we are, whose life am I leading and why. It was a starter's pistol, adapted. Did you know that?"

"Yes."

"Yes, she said. You are well informed, he exclaimed. Where is the check, they inquired."

She smiled a bit at that. Progress, he thought. It wasn't macabre, perhaps, but it had a little something all its own.

6

Pammy was writing a direct-mail piece on the subjects of sorrow and death. The point was to get people to send for a Grief Management brochure entitled "It Ends For Him On The Day He Dies—But You Have To Face Tomorrow." The brochure

elaborated on death, defined the study known as grief management and offered a detailed summary of the company's
programs ("Let Professionals Help You Cope") and a listing
of regional offices. It cost a dollar.

Pammy had written the brochure months earlier. Ethan, in
one of his moments of feigned grandeur, had called it "a classic of dispassion and tact." There were others in the office who
considered it too "nuts-and-boltsy," like a four-page insert for
radio condensers in some dealer publication.

"Death is a religious experience," Ethan had said. "It is also
nuts-and-boltsy. Something fails to work, you die. A de-
monstrable consequence."

In a context in which every phrase can take on horribly
comic significance, she thought she'd done well. Her job, in
the main, was a joke, as was the environment in which she
carried it out. But she was proud of that brochure. She'd main-
tained a sensible tone. There was a fact in nearly every sentence. She hadn't let them print on tint. If people wanted to
merchandise anguish and death, and if others wished to have
their suffering managed for them, everybody could at least go
about it with a measure of discretion and taste.

"Say it, say it."

"Maine."

"Again," he said. "Please, now, hurry, God, mercy."

"Maine," she said. "Maine."

There was activity on the floor. Lyle left post 5 and stopped
at the Bell teleprinter. A young male carrier went by, blond
shoulder-length hair. Lyle pressed the E key, then GM. Feed
him to Ethan. Paper slid along the floor before settling. There
was a second level of noise, very brief, a clubhouse cheer. He

stepped back to get a look at the visitors' gallery. Attractive woman standing behind the bulletproof glass. He looked at the print-out as he walked back to his booth. Range for the day. Numbers clicked onto the enunciator board. Eat, eat. Shit, eat, shit. Feed her to us in decimals. Aggress, enfoul, decrete. Eat, eat, eat.

$$V.R. \quad GM—12.33 \quad 2524$$

$$106.400$$
$$10.10 \quad 69$$
$$12.30 \quad 70$$
$$10.12 \quad 68\frac{1}{2}$$
$$12.33 \quad +70 + 1\frac{1}{2}$$

He went to the smoking area, where he saw Frank Mc-Kechnie standing at the edge of a noisy group, biting skin from his thumb. Lyle isolated two members of the group and began doing a routine from a comedy record he'd recently bought. It was something he felt he did particularly well. It suited his careful stance, the neutral way his eyes recorded an audience. He could read their delight at his self-containment, the incongruity of enclosed humor. They began to lean. They actually watched his lips. When a third member of the group edged in, drawn by the laughter, Lyle ended prematurely and went over to McKechnie, who looked off into the smoke that rose above the gathering.

"So where are we?"

"Who knows?"

"We're inside," Lyle said.

"That's for sure."

"It's obvious."

"It's obvious because if we were outside the cars would be climbing up my back."

"The outside world."

"That's it," McKechnie said. "Things that happen and you're helpless. All you can do is wait for how bad."

Lyle didn't know exactly what they were talking about. He exchanged this kind of dialogue with McKechnie often. He'd watch his friend carefully throughout. McKechnie seemed to take it seriously. He gave the impression he knew what they were talking about.

"I want to ask you about this man who shot Sedbauer."

"Huge page in today's paper."

"Sedbauer's guest."

McKechnie made a motion with his thumb and index finger, indicating a headline.

"Mystery of Stock Exchange Murder Unraveling Slowly."

"So far I like it."

"Gunman, obscure background, dum dum dum, carrying, get this, a bomb on his person, dum dum. Suspected terrorist network. Confusion over identity. Links being sought, dumdy dum. The guy refuses to talk, see a lawyer or leave his cell."

"He had a bomb *when* on his person?"

"When he was caught. After he shot George. He was standing right over there. A miniature explosive package. I quote."

"Nice."

"Where are we, Lyle, as you put it so beautifully yourself?"

"We're inside."

"Where do we want to be?"

"Inside."

"Those both are right answers."

"I prepared."

"Wait and see how bad," McKechnie said. "That's all you can do. I'm getting ready to raise the barricades. There's a serious health problem in the family. There's my brother piling up gambling debts and making midnight phone calls complete with whispering and little sobs. Bookies, loan sharks, threats. Very educational. Interest compounded hourly. Then there's my oldest, who has a hearing problem to begin with and now out of nowhere who's found sitting on the floor in his room just staring at the wall. Twice last week. Has trouble moving his arms. Doesn't want to talk. He's too young to take drugs. It's not drugs. We had him to the doctor. They did these scans they do. Nothing definite. So now we're thinking of a shrink for kids. Did you ever feel you were in a vise? I walk around thinking what happened."

"Let's try to have lunch next week."

McKechnie reduced his cigarette butt to a speck of tobacco and a speck of paper. He dropped these on the floor. Then he jumped about a foot in the air, landing on the specks.

"Enjoy that?"

"Very advanced," Lyle said.

"I used to be better. You should have seen me."

"It's something you couldn't do in the outside world. They'd point and say ya ya."

"Why don't we have lunch right now as a matter of fact? We'll go upstairs."

"I don't eat up there anymore."

"Why not?"

"I don't know, Frank."

"There has to be a reason."

"I suppose."

"You don't know what it is."

"I just haven't been up there in a while."

"Lyle, I'm not exactly a promoter of tight-ass social customs. I don't have decanters full of sherry that I wheel out for my guests with their Bentleys parked outside. But there's nothing wrong with eating at the Exchange. It's halfway civilized and that's something."

"It's inside."

"It's inside, right. It's convenient, it's quick, it's good, it's nice and it's halfway fucking gracious, which is no small feat these days. So stop being stupid. You're talking like a jerk."

"No pissa me off, Frank."

Pammy had dinner with Ethan and Jack. They went to a place in SoHo. She was excited. Dinner out. Somewhere in her waking awareness there were glints of anticipation whenever Ethan and Jack walked into a room or when she picked up the ringing phone and it was one of them on the other end. Most people in her life were dispiriting presences. She looked forward to being with these two. If Ethan ever left his job, she'd sink into stupor and mutism.

The restaurant was full of hanging plants. A young woman arrived with the wine, telling them their food order would be delayed.

"There's a smoky fire in the basement right now. The kitchen staff is down there arguing over whether or not they want to pee on it. I opted out, unless they rig a swing, I told them. Distance is not my thing. There's Peter Hearn the conceptualist and his dog Alfalfa. I can never uncork without rupturing myself in the worst places, unless you don't consider sex important. Do you ever see how they uncork, with the knees? I'm sorry but I refuse to do that. It's degrading. I give a little bend, which is gruesome enough. More than that, forget about, you'll have to go somewhere else."

They started on the wine. Smoke seeped into the main room but nobody left. There was no food being served. Everybody felt obliged to crack jokes and to drink a little faster than usual. A situation such as this could not be allowed to evolve without comic remarks and a trace of sophisticated hysteria. Ethan's mouth slid gradually into a secret grin. A woman at the other end of the room coughed and waved a handkerchief. Jack took the empty wine bottle to the waitress, who returned eventually with another, which Jack opened. Pammy wondered if her face was blotched. Wine did that. The man with the coughing woman ordered another round. Another man came out of the basement and began carrying plants out the front door. A two-inch needle, a sect ornament of some kind, was embedded in the flesh beneath his lower lip, pointing downward, its angle of entry about forty-five degrees. Jack hit the table and looked away, trying to suppress his laughter. The man left plants on the sidewalk and came back in for more. Wine squirted out of Jack's mouth. The room was filling with smoke. There was noise in the street, then wide beams of interweaving light. About ten firemen walked in. Pammy started to laugh, chewing at the air, her face blazing and clear, transcendently sane in this rose-stone glow. The firemen waddled around, bumping into each other. Ethan finished off another glass. The room seemed physically diminished by their entrance. They were outsized in helmets and boots, stepping heavily, lifting themselves like men on skis. Pammy couldn't stop laughing. The firemen cleared the place, slowly. Everybody was coughing, bottles and glasses in their hands. They trooped out, disappointed at the lack of applause.

It was dark. There were two hundred people in the streeet. Jack stepped onto the narrow platform at the back of one of the fire engines. He swung out from the vertical bar. The gaiety they'd brought into the street dissolved in minutes. Ethan and Pam started off down the block but Jack didn't want to get off the fire truck. He shouted commands and made wailing noises. Nobody paid much attention. The man with the needle beneath his lip came out with the last of the plants. Firemen dragged a hose around the corner. Ethan stood looking at Jack, a steadying distance in his gaze.

"I wonder what happened to the rain they predicted," Pammy said.

Jack came along finally. They turned a corner and headed south, moving toward Canal Street and the possibility of a taxi. Standing outside the cast-iron buildings were large cardboard cylinders that contained industrial sweepings from the factory lofts. Jack charged one of them, shoulder-first, knocking it down. They followed along quietly as he ranged both sides of the street, crashing into containers. Just past Grand he hurdled an overturned container and veered neatly, forearm out front, body set low, to run into a metal garbage can. Pammy, eventually, noted that Ethan hadn't altered stride and she had to hurry to catch up with him. Jack was sitting in the gutter, holding his knee. The can was on its side, rolling only slightly back and forth, much of its contents still within, an indication of weight. To Pammy it made sense in a way. He'd always appeared to have reserves of uncommitted energy. A hitter of garbage cans. She watched him get to his feet, raggedly. Although there was no sign of an empty cab, Ethan leaned into the sparse traffic, arm high in the air.

"Does he do this often?"

"Tuesdays and Thursdays," Ethan said. "The rest of the week he speaks in tongues."

Lyle sometimes carried yellow teleprinter slips with him for days. He saw in the numbers and stock symbols an artful reduction of the external world to printed output, the machine's coded model of exactitude. One second of study, a glance was all it took to return to him an impression of reality disconnected from the resonance of its own senses. Aggression was refined away, the instinct to possess. He saw fractions, decimal points, plus and minus signs. A picture of the competitive mechanism of the world, of greasy teeth engaging on the rim of a wheel, was nowhere in evidence. The paper contained nerve impulses: a synaptic digit, a phoneme, a dimensionless point. He knew that people want to see their own spittle dripping from the lacy openwork of art. On the slip of paper in his hand there was no intimation of lives defined by the objects around them, morbid tiers of immortality. Inked figures were all he saw. This was property in its own right, tucked away, his particular share (once removed) of the animal body breathing in the night.

When Pammy got home, he wasn't there. This was disappointing. Lately she'd found that the nutritive material for their sex life was often provided by others, whoever happened to be present at a party or other gathering. She wondered whether she'd become too complex to care whether the others were gay or straight. It would be nice, so nice if he walked in right now. When she realized how late it was, she grew angry. Soon she was doing what she always did when she was mad at Lyle. She began to clean the apartment. First she mopped the kitchen, then the bathroom. She swept up in the living room and, once the kitchen floor was dry, quickly did the dishes. It was an intricate cycle of expiation and virtue, a return to self-discipline. Whenever things went badly between them, she took it as a preview, seeing herself alone in a brilliantly well-kept apartment, everything in place, everything *white* somehow, a sense of iron-fisted independence clearly apparent in all this organization. In the middle of the night, obviously too late to vacuum, she took a shower, put on her pajamas and sat reading in bed, feeling good about herself.

Lyle came home.

"Your face is splotched," he said.

"You'll get hit."

"What are you doing up? You're still up. It's unbelievably late. I've never seen it so late. It's really late out there. You should see. Go to the window and look. No, don't. You won't learn a thing that way. Stay where you are."

"He feels like talking."

"I was downtown. I walked around down there till now. What was it like, she asked. Well, to begin with, it was cool finally, a rivery breeze, and no one around, nothing, a drunk or two early on but later nothing, a car, another car, another car, looking for the tunnel. The district, outwardly, is like the end of organized time—outwardly, mind you. At night I mean it's like somebody forgot something. They went away. The mystery, right, of why everybody left these gorgeous pueblos."

"Inwardly?"

"Things happening. Little men in eyeshades."

"Fascinating, these insights of his."

"What is it, Splotch? Annoyed at my lack of consideration? I called. You weren't here."

"We ought to go out more."

"There's nothing out there. That's my point. Everybody went away. You can hear doors blowing shut in the wind. The scientists are mystified."

7

Lyle cultivated a quality of self-command. As a corollary to this extreme presence of mind, he built a space between himself and most of the people he was likely to deal with in the course of daily events. He was aware of his studied passage down the corridors of his firm's offices. Happily he parodied his own manner, swiveling toward a face and beaming an anemic look right past it. It was satisfying to stand on the floor, say, during a lull in trading, or after hours in a bar in the district, and note how some people subtly exhibited their relative closeness to him while others, sensing his apartness or knowing it for fact, were diligent in keeping ritual distances.

The waiter, at six feet four, let his head slip down a notch as he took their orders.

"I want something outer spacelike," Lyle said. "What's a zombie? Bring me one of those."

Rosemary Moore had a Scotch and water. Her boss, Larry Zeltner, ordered gin and tonic for himself and also for the two young women, known to Lyle only as Jackie and Gail. He'd come upon them in the elevator as he and Rosemary were leaving the office. Zeltner suggested they all go for a drink. Lyle quickly agreed, trying to indicate that he and Rosemary had entered the elevator together by chance, just as the others had.

"It's what I said this morning," Zeltner said. "It's what I always say: who'll do it? Get somebody to do it and I'm with you. Otherwise goodbye. Then there's the situation, how do we total, who's reconciling, where do you tighten up the indicators?"

Lyle made a point of conversing with Jackie, who was unattractive. He didn't know why he took this precaution or what, exactly, it meant. Somehow it seemed a safe course. He finished his drink before the others were halfway through with theirs. Jackie appeared to be studying him as she spoke, measuring his attentiveness or wondering why his replies had dwindled to simple nods of the head, three every ten seconds. Rosemary said she had to leave. He emptied his face of indications. Zeltner told her not to bother with money; it was his treat, et cetera. Lyle watched her walk out the door. She hadn't implied to the others, in any manner at all, that she'd ever spoken a word to him before this evening. He wasn't sure whether this was by specific design or part of a social code that prevailed in all her relations with others.

"Yumpin' yimminy," he said. "My train to catch. Have to go out to the boonies to see this friend of mine's wife with all kinds of problems. Jesus, hospitals, I hate them. Kid is all screwed up. Wife may be serious. I told him I'd be out tonight. Larry, lunch, without fail, the soonest."

He smiled at the women, left money and hurried out, trying to detach himself from the tiny disaster of that speech. It was rush hour in the streets. He half ran toward the corner where the Volkswagen usually arrived to get her. His body was filled with chemical activity, streams of desperate elation. She was still there, waiting. Again he could see his lips moving as he spoke through a hole in the air. Rosemary put her sunglasses on.

They were in a taxi heading uptown. Strategically he'd chosen a bar near the approach to the Queensboro Bridge. It seemed the way to deal with her. She was the kind of woman whose very lack of reaction summoned in him a need to resort to discredited tactics. The driver's name was Wolodymyr Koltowski. Lyle tried to ignore the hack number. He was sweating extensively. Traffic on the East River Drive was unusually manic-depressive, a careening streak of excitation and suicidal gloom. Lyle felt at fault, as he always did in a cab, with a woman, when traffic moved too slowly or at this raging pace. He realized he'd forgotten to put stamps on some envelopes the night before.

The place was crowded. There were no empty tables and they couldn't get near the bar. He didn't know this area well. He didn't know what was around. It had been there all day, this unfinished space, a negative awareness. He reached in for their drinks and worked his way toward her. She stood near the door, legs crossed at the ankles. He'd meant to put stamps on the envelopes. There were bills inside. He'd written the checks and wanted to get them in the mail. To pay a bill was to seal off the world. The pleasure here was inward-tending, an accumulation of self. Putting stamps on the envelopes was the decisive point. Stamps were emblems of authentication. Her hands were folded in front of her, purse dangling from her wrist. Wolodymyr Koltowski. Shut up, he told himself. The crowd at the bar continued to grow, pressing out toward them. Rosemary didn't seem to mind.

It was a challenge to something deeper than virility. To be recognized by this woman, accepted as a distinct and welcome presence in her murky ken, was the end toward which his passions were now directed.

They rode out over the bridge and onto Queens Boulevard. They got out of the cab and walked north half a block. It was still light. She lived on the ground floor of a row house with a corrugated aluminum awning outside and webbed beach chairs stacked in the hallway.

There were three small rooms and a large kitchen. Until he wandered into the kitchen he saw nothing he might identify with Rosemary as occupant of the place—Rosemary Moore as opposed to someone he'd never seen before, or talked to, or wanted to touch, another woman entirely, or a man dressed as a woman, snatching him out of a dark hallway into this square bag of space, these shades of gray and beige. There was no feeling of individual history, the narrative in things, habits intact in one's belongings.

In the kitchen he stood before a large corkboard. Pinned there were ticket stubs, menus, matchbook covers, photos of Rosemary with various people. The echoes of her self-absorption converged here, apparently. In one photo she sat on a sofa between two men. There was no one else in the picture but Lyle suspected that others (besides the photographer) were present in the room. One man's sidelong glance, the other's half-sheepish mien indicated the possibility of on-lookers. The man being sheepish was George Sedbauer, heavy-set and balding. Lyle had seen news photos of him after the shooting. Of course he'd also seen him dead, although he wouldn't have been able to identify Sedbauer from those scat-tered glimpses on the floor. Rosemary handed him a drink. It had only two ice cubes in it. It wouldn't be cold enough. He wanted a cold drink. He realized, incredibly, that he'd forgot-ten what he was going to ask her. He had to work his way back to it.

"That's George, isn't it?"

"Yes."

"Who's with him?"

"That's me in the middle. That's somebody Vilas or Vilar. I think it was on a weekend. We went to Lake Placid? It was supposed to be to ski. That's the lobby where we stayed. Or that's the room. I think that was someone's room."

"Who's somebody Vilas?"

"That's the man who shot George."

"Interesting," he remarked.

"He was around a lot sometimes. Other times you never saw him for long periods."

"I think that's interesting, said the wide-eyed young man."

"George didn't ski. That was it. When we got all the way up there, George hated snow."

Unsure of something, she'd narrow her eyes and gaze into space. She gestured slowly. Her face betrayed the barest aban-donment when she turned to find him staring. It was necessary, he knew, to talk to her about herself. She was tall, more pale than fair, walking in a somber frost.

To be alone with her was to occupy the immediate center of things. There were no gradations to this kind of desire. Everything turned on the point of her chalk image. It would be essential to talk awhile. He would find his way to her through this process of filling in.

"This drink needs about eleven more ice cubes."

"I don't think you can stay too long."

"Let's sit in the living room. I'm a living-room fanatic. I'm a buff, really. I have this thing. Without a living room around I'm dead, just about."

The sensual pleasure of banality was a subject worth the deepest investigation. He lingered in the kitchen to watch her walk into the next room. He sat facing her, ten feet away, knowing she would cross her legs. There were cigarettes and liquor, absolute necessities when he was with her. He tried to limit his remarks to tapered extensions of predictable types. He was working toward a pure state, some embryonic science of desire, perhaps to be known as reciprocal hypnotism. When she spoke he concentrated every effort on creating a face that would return to her not only a sense of what she'd said but of the person speaking, Rosemary Moore in a camisole dress. He moved to the sofa, settling in next to her. Together they would craft the branding instrument of character.

"When I was flying," she said, "I was always sleeping too little or too much. I used to sleep whole days sometimes. This is a little more regular. But I don't know how interesting it'll wind up being. There isn't enough to do. I have to see if I'm going to stay. The people are pretty nice, though. Not like this job with buyers that I had. That was insane. They would shout into the phone. I don't like when people *do* that."

He took the glass out of her hand and put it on the end table next to his own drink. She moved her head briefly, shaking hair out of her eyes or ending one sequence of encounter to begin another. The second he touched her, touch turned to grip.

8

Pammy put tap shoes and tights into her shoulder bag. The class was on West Fourteenth Street, two evenings a week, eight-thirty to ten. In charge was Nan Fryer, a woman with brittle hair and a scar across one side of her jaw. There were as many as forty people there some nights. The studio was rented from a theater group called Dynamic Tranquillity. Nan was a member of the group and she attributed her prowess in tap to ethical systems of discipline.

"Hop, you're not hopping. Shuf-*ful*, shuf-*ful*."

Pammy danced before a mirror at the back of the room. Her body was suited to tights, one of the few such bodies in evidence. She was practicing a routine that involved a precarious off-balance change. Pammy loved tap. She had dancing feet, it appeared. A born hoofer. Arms flung up, toes crackling, heels beating out a series of magnetic stresses, she repeatedly sought a particular cadence, the single instance of lucidity that would lift her into some dizzy sphere of ecstasy and sweat. Tap was so crisp when done correctly, so pleasing to one's sense of the body as a coordinated organism able to make its own arithmetic.

Nan Fryer clapped her hands, bringing the tapping to a halt. People drooped somewhat, bodies throbbing. The men in class were dressed variously, from track suits to routine casual wear. Most of the women wore tights or flared slacks. Nan walked among them, talking. She wore silver shoes, cut-off jeans and a Dynamic Tranquillity T-shirt. It was an outfit that made her facial scar appear all the more tragic.

"I like your breathing. You're all breathing so well. This is important in that we're concerned with movement and the forces affecting movement. There are areas and awarenesses in you that tap makes accessible. You are accessible to yourself. Notice how calm you're getting. Little by little, deeper and deeper. Unblock your nervous systems. Believe in your breathing. This is so essential to getting the most out of tap. When I first came to tap, I thought it was just a ticky tacky dance. It can be so much more. Movement and force. Force and energy. Energy and peace. You are a free person for the first time in that your whole body is aware of the physical and moral universe."

Pammy looked out a window at the back of the room. Traffic moved swiftly. There were flushes of sunset in a glass door across the street, a bargain shop. Her hands were over her ears.

"Okay, kids, crossover time."

The rest of the session Pammy danced intently, cracking down on her heels, definitive contact. She worked awhile on the intermediate routine, step number two, moving sideways

across the face of the mirror to confront a radiator and pipes.
Nan played an old show tune on the phonograph and danced
a set of advanced combinations. The students formed a circle
around her. Soon they were all dancing, trying to duplicate
the complex floor patterns, tapping, swaying, elbowing out
into some private space to strut awhile, quietly, on the hard-
wood floor.

"Do not tight-*ten*. Com-plete loose-ness. Re-lax ank-les, Ar-
nold Mas-low, do not tight-*ten*."

Lyle stood in a phone booth in Grand Central waiting for
McKechnie to pick up and watching people heading for their
trains, skidding along, their shoulders collapsed—a day's
work, a drink or two causing subtle destruction, a rumpling
beyond the physical, all moving through constant sourceless
noise, mouths slightly open, the fish of cities.

"You're sure it's not too late."

"Lyle, say what you want to say."

"The other day we talked about George Sedbauer. Who
shot him, so on, so forth. Well remember you mentioned this
secretary of Zeltner's one time? She knows a little about this. I
got to know her a little. She first of all knew Sedbauer. She
knew the man or knows the man who shot him. That's the key
thing. There's a photograph. I saw it. And she knows about
the gun, what kind of gun, but the gun she could have read in
the paper. The key thing is the man who did the shooting. She
knows him. Should somebody be told about this? Or what,
Frank?"

"You saw this picture."

"They were in it. George, her, the guy. Unless she's invent-
ing. But why would she invent?"

"I want you to talk to a friend of mine," McKechnie said. "I'll have him get in touch with you. Yeah, we'd better do that."

Ethan and Jack came over the next evening with meat loaf leftovers. They all went up to the roof, where management had laid slate over the tar and provided four picnic tables (chained to the walls) and several evergreen shrubs in large planters. Lyle arrived last, carrying drinks on a tray.

"I didn't know this was up here," Jack said.

"It's to give Pammy a look at the World Trade Center whenever she's depressed. That gets her going again."

"I want to drink something classic," Ethan said. "None of this tequila business. What is that, tequila? I've decided to live after all. No more poison pinwheels."

"A bit of poetry, that," Pammy said. "Here, somebody serve. Give me a small piece. Are we eating or drinking? I'm confused and we're just getting started."

"What's that?" Jack said. "Is that the Municipal Building? Is that, what, the Woolworth Building? You can't see that far from here, can you?"

"If you'd brought wine I could give you something classic. I could give you wine."

"We brought meat loaf. Who else brings meat loaf?"

"You left the wine in the cab, I take it, from past experience."

"We had this cabdriver coming up here," Jack said. "No spikka da English too good. Tried to come up here via Chinatown."

"Ah so."

"Threats of bodily harm," Ethan said.

"Who's what here? I'd like some bread with this. No, I wouldn't. Forget that. Cancel that order, waiter. I'm a dancer now. Austerity is my life. What's it called—an austere regimen. I will accept a drink, however, if one of you turdnagels will pass me a glass, being careful at all times, these being new and extremely high-priced drinking vessels."

"This salad's fabulous."

"Thank you, Jack."

"A salad among salads," Ethan said.

"Lyle tossed it."

"Loud and prolonged applause."

"I tossed it."

"Meaning to ask, Lyle, what's happening on the street?"

"The street of streets."

"Have you been declared officially antiquated or what? Are you viable, Lyle? We all want to know. Will there be a floor to trade on in the near future? Or does it all pass into the mists of history, ladies and gentlemen, and you are there."

"I vote for the mists of history. But who knows, really? There's an awful strong argument for the membership's point of view. But the current's the other way."

"Really, you'd haul it all down?"

"It's not hauling it down. It's opening it up. Of course you don't know exactly what it is you're opening up. That's the trouble with currents."

"They can take you right over the falls."

"Right over the falls and your barrel too."

"Should we be worried?" Ethan said.

"Pick an opening and move right in. That's the only, you know, method of, whatever—maintaining some kind of self-

determination, a specific presence. Out into the streets, clerks
of history, package-wrappers. Freedom, freedom."

"You've learned your lesson well, Spartacus."

It was nearly dark. Lyle went down for more liquor and ice.
He dialed Rosemary's number. No one answered. In the
kitchen he moved past a glass cabinet and realized there was a
flaw in his likeness. Something unfamiliar in the middle of his
face. At the same time he felt dampness there. He went into
the bathroom. It was his nose, bleeding. He held some tissue
there until the flow diminished. Then he put a box of Kleenex
on the tray, along with tequila, vodka, bitter lemon and ice,
and went back up to the roof. Someone was at one of the other
tables. It was a small boy wearing a straw fedora. He stood
against the chair, eyes averted. Lyle sensed that the others
were watching him to measure the comic dimensions of his
reaction to the boy. He walked toward them, looking out over
the umbrella that was set into the table. Deliberately he placed
the tray down, moving objects out of the way with calculated
disdain. They waited for him to say something. He sat, moving
slowly as possible. His nose started bleeding again. This became the joke, of course. It was funnier than anything he
could have said. He inserted a tissue in his nostril and let it
hang there, his expression one of weary forbearance.

"His mother left him," Jack said. "She'd come right back.
You leave kids on roofs?"

"He's a forties kid," Pammy said.

"But that hat, I can't believe."

"He's a forties kid. He's got a two-toned little suit. I bet he
never grows up. He'll stay three feet something. He'll smoke a
little pipe and never go anywhere without that hat and two-

toned suit. His name will be Bert Follett and I'd like to marry him. I'd also like a white wine with club soda please."

"Where am I supposed to get it?"

"Wherever it is. It exists, that's all. Existentially you should be able to get it."

"She's such a snarly nymphet," Ethan said. "Isn't she at times? In the office they fear her on sight."

"Oh, she's a proper moll, she is."

"Take the Kleenex out of your nose."

"Nose, what, who . . . he trailed off."

They finished the meat loaf. Pammy went over to talk to the boy. They had a pleasant conversation about dogs in the neighborhood. Her attentions made him glow a little. She felt he was aware of the whole scene, not just their talk. He was enjoying *himself* as part of it. Child among adults. Cute suit. The ambiance. His mother came to take him away and Pammy rejoined the others.

"I'm saying this is it," Lyle said, "and we don't know what it means. It's collapsed right in on us. It's ahead of schedule. Look who's back looking a little sick about something. It's backed into us. It's here."

"Vales of time and space."

"If I had a mother like that," Jack said, "I'd hang around on rooftops too. I do anyway, hubba hubba."

"What is this, tequila?" Ethan said. "I don't want this. Take it away, someone. If this is tequila and if I'm drinking it, there's something seriously amiss."

"That plane looks like it's going to hit."

"I think I'm sick, guys."

"I wanted so very much for us to be brilliant together this evening."

"I think I may blow my cookies any minute."

"I was sure it would hit," Jack said.

"I don't want to blame the meat loaf but there's something happening in my stomach that's not supposed to."

"She's going to blow her cookies, Lyle. Get her out of here."

"If we had something brilliant to drink perhaps. Too long I've accepted second best."

"Lyle, you smoke? I didn't know you smoked. When did you start smoking?"

In the bathroom mirror he watched the blood seep out. It was pretty in a way. It came so slowly, an idealized flow, no sense at all of some impelling force. He watched it fill the indentation above his lip. The color of his blood intrigued him, its meaty bloom, a near sheen of the gayest sap imaginable. He held his head back, finally, until the bleeding stopped, then went into the kitchen, where Pammy stood before the steaming basin. He opened the refrigerator, pressing her against the sink as he did so, an offhand attempt to annoy, not even mildly riling, and lifted out a jar of olives.

"How come no dishwasher?"

"I want these glasses to know what it feels like to be washed by human hands," she said. "I don't want them to grow up thinking everything's done the easy way, by machine, with impersonal detergent."

"It's broke again?"

"You call."

"You, for once."

"I called the other."

"I'm not calling. I don't care. Let it be broke."

"Don't call. We won't call. I don't care."

"I'm serious," he said. "I don't care."

"I won't be here, so."

"Neither will I except in and out."

She made a prissy face and delivered a distorted version of his tone of voice.

"Neither will I except in and out."

After the close Lyle showed up at the office. She wasn't at her desk. He lingered in the area, trying to be inconspicuous. Deciding finally that she'd left early or hadn't come in at all, he went into an empty office and called her at home. She didn't answer. Three times, at ten-minute intervals, he returned to dial her number. On the elevator he thought: *grieved suitor.* Was he coming to understand the motivating concepts that led to obsession, despair, crimes of passion? Haw haw haw. Denial and assertion. The trap of wanting. The blessedness of being wronged. What sweet vistas it opens, huge neurotic landscapes, what exemptions. Gaw damn, Miss Molly. In the taxi he was oddly calm. He had the driver take him two blocks past his destination. (It was that kind of involvement, already.) He called her number from a booth near a gas station. When she didn't answer he walked to the house and rang her bell in the vestibule. He waited there an hour, then went back to the phone booth. There was no answer. He thought he saw the VW turn into her street. He ran across Queens Boulevard and hurried to the corner. The car was parked in front of her building. It was still early, at least two hours of sunlight left. He smoked and waited. A man and a woman (not Rosemary) came out of the building. The car moved north. He went to the house and pressed her bell again. No one came to the door. He remained in the vestibule half an hour, ringing and waiting. Then he went to the booth near the gas station and dialed her number. There was no answer. He waited five minutes and dialed again. Then he decided to count to fifty. At fifty he would call one last time. When she didn't answer, he lowered the count to twenty-five.

Pammy in the back of a rented limousine sat drinking from a Thermos bottle full of gin and dry vermouth. When the car passed a delicatessen near the Midtown Tunnel she asked the driver to stop. She ran inside and bought a lemon. She came running out, in high boots and a puffy cap, her getaway gear. Back in the car she tore off a strip of lemon rind with her teeth and thumbnail. She rubbed it over the inner edge of the Thermos cup, then dropped it in. If she had to fly, she would do it at less than total consciousness. She drank much faster than usual. It was roughly eight parts gin to one vermouth. She didn't like martinis particularly but felt they represented a certain flamboyant abandon, at least in theory—a devil-may-care quality that suited a trip to the airport. If she had to go to the airport at all, she would go in a limousine, wearing high boots, faded denims and a street kid's jive cap. She knew she looked pretty terrific. She also knew Ethan and Jack would enjoy her story of going out to the airport, smashed, in a mile-long limo, although she had to admit she disliked hearing other people go on about their drinking or drug-taking, the quantities involved, the comic episodes that ensued. But they'd be glad to see her and they'd love her outfit. She felt so good, leaving. Maine was up there somewhere, vast miles of granite and pine. She could see Jack's face when she walked into the arrivals area, hear Ethan's arch greeting. It would be a separation from the world of legalities and claims, an edifying loss of definition. She poured another cup. When the land began to flatten and empty out, she knew they were in the vicinity of the airport. It was a landscape that acceded readily to a sense of pre-emption. She lowered the shades on the side windows and rode the rest of the way in semidarkness, conscientiously sipping from the cup.

Lyle was slightly surprised by the degree to which he enjoyed being alone. Everything was put away, all the busy spill of conjugal habits. He walked through the apartment, noting lapsed boundaries, a modification of sight lines and planes. Of course it hadn't nearly the same warmth. But there was something else, an airy span about the place, the re-distancing of objects about a common point. Things were less abrupt and sundry. There was an evenness of feeling, a radial symmetry involving not so much his body and the rooms through which he passed but an inner presence and its sounding lines, the secret possibilities of self. He'd seen her, after he stepped off the bus, come out of the building and walk to the limousine. He was half a block away. She'd stood briefly on the sidewalk, checking her shoulder bag for tickets, keys, so forth. The long boots were a surprise, and the hat as well, making her seem, even from this distance, never more captivating, physically, a striking sight really, and vulnerable, as people can appear to be who are fetching and carefree and unaware of being watched. He felt his soul swing to a devastating tenderness. She was innocent there, that moment; had put away guile and chosen to distrust experience. Short of pretending to be blind, he could do nothing but succumb to love. The bronze shock of it was pure truth, the kind that reveals conditions within, favors and old graces coming into the light. He watched the automobile glide into traffic. He shared her going, completely. It would be only several weeks but in that time he knew the simplest kitchen implement would be perceived as brighter, more distinct, an object of immediate experience. Their separations were intense.

9

He passed McKechnie several times on the floor but said nothing, as was customary, and avoided eye contact. He looked for him during slack periods and again in the smoking area. That night he called him at home.

"Frank, a friend of yours was supposed to get in touch with me."

"I told him the thing."

"Who is he, where is he, when do we talk?"

"I don't know what he does but he does it in Langley, Virginia."

"Which means what?"

"Christ, Lyle."

" 'Christ, Lyle.' What's that? 'Christ, Lyle.' "

"Use your head," McKechnie said.

"Look, just tell me, will you?"

"Langley fucking Virginia."

"What is that? 'Langley fucking Virginia.' What *is* that?"

"Don't be stupid. You're being intentionally stupid."

"Is there a curse attached if you utter the goddamn thing? What happens, your eyeballs drop out?"

"Shit but you're dumb sometimes."

"Langley, Virginia."

"That's right."

"When do I hear?"

"Don't ask me."

"This is supposed to be some kind of obscure figure and everybody's searching for terrorist links and here's this secretary walking around who's met the man, who knows him apparently, who's got his picture hanging in her kitchen. It could be important, Frank."

"Not to me it couldn't."

"You don't even know what he does, your friend."

"I don't know, that's right."

"And you don't want to know."

"Never righter, Lyle."

"But he does it in Langley, Virginia."

"Wow but you're stupid."

"Say it, Frank."

"Either you know or you don't. If you don't know, try guessing."

"I want to hear you say it."

"Try guessing."

"Utter it, come on."

"I'm hanging up," McKechnie said.

"Whisper it in my ear."

"I'm putting down the phone, dumbfuck."

10

Rosemary's flesh, her overample thighs, the contact chill of her body were the preoccupations of his detachment from common bonds. Once her clothes were off, she rarely spoke. He gripped and bit at her, leaving spit everywhere. Her breath was milky. She was uninterested in all but the most common-place sex. Suitable, he thought. Perfectly acceptable. Why not? She clutched the back of his neck. Her flesh obsessed him, color and touch, bland odors coming off it. She might almost have been a drugged child. He wanted to scratch at her flesh, to leave teeth marks, pink ridges, alternately lapping and claw-ing away. It was hardly the mood of squandered afternoons. He wanted to put his mouth inside hers; roar.

"It's that I'm all through with that. I'm out. Let it all come down. Don't you think everybody, nearly, feels that way about their work, where they work all those years? It's insane, be-sides. The whole thing is. Besides, why not?"

She never let him undress her. She would go into the bath-room, emerging ten minutes later, slightly ill at ease although not about her nakedness, he felt, but about the way she walked when barefoot, a somehow downhill step, heavy-

tending. She showed little sign of whatever measures of desire
his own body might have been expected to arouse in her.

"There may be some people you can meet."

"Of course, I know."

"I was wondering," she said. "The car?"

"Sure, I remember, clearly."

"That picks me up from work sometimes."

"Absolutely, who else but them?"

"If you want to."

"Why not, certainly, what am I here for?"

Her thighs distorted the line of her body. A plodder's thighs,
surprisingly. Hard to spot in someone who wears a dress but
reassuring in that it confounded the set of his expectations. He
pressed onto her constantly, all his body, ravenous for flesh,
his hands mixing and working her into a mass of mild discol-
oration. She never approached orgasm. He accepted this not
as a deficiency he might correct (as people often interpret the
matter), using patience and skill, the bed mechanic's experience; nor as a deeper exhaustion, a failure of the spirit. It was
simply part of their dynamics, the condition of being together,
and he had no intention of altering the elements of the spell or
even of wishing them otherwise. One kind of sex or another
was not the question. The triteness that pervaded their meetings supplied what he wanted of eroticism and made "one" or
"the other" a question of recondite semantics. He gripped her
fiercely. There was never any point at which he guided himself
past a certain stage or prepared to approach a culmination. It
was too disorganized, the moments of intensity only loosely
foreseen. He would climax unexpectedly, barely aware, feeling
both criminal and naïve.

She is padding to the bathroom, he thought. Holding her breasts she admires her body in the full-length mirror. She is rosy with fulfillment. Two waiting-maids enter to prepare her perfumed bath. On the bed of carved walnut, he thought, her lover reclines against a mound of silk pillows, recalling how she'd groaned with pleasure.

TWO

1

She turned the car into a dead-end street. It was Sunday and very still, midafternoon. Lyle looked out the side window, dreamily, his arm hanging out over the door, a surfer returning from a day at the beach. The woman parked, turned off the ignition and sat there. Lyle waited. Only one sidewalk was paved. The house was gray frame, two-storied, fronted by shrubs and a single tree. She made a small noise, routine irritation, as she attempted to bend herself out of the car. She looked back in at Lyle, who hadn't yet reached for the door.

"I forgot the Cheerios," she said. "This will precipitate a small crisis in the morning. Is that right—'precipitate'?"

"I think so," he said. "Maybe not quite."

She reached in for the groceries.

"Do I come in now?" he said. "Or wait out here."

"Oh, I think come in. By all means now. I think it's clearly the thing."

He heard piano music coming from the back of the house, a record player apparently, upper floor. The woman, reacting to the sound, turned on the radio. She gestured to Lyle and he sat in a deep chair with enormous laminated arms. The woman, Marina Vilar, stood behind the table the radio was on, reaching over the top of the radio to turn the station selector. Through the window behind her Lyle could see part of a bridge, either the Whitestone or the Throgs Neck. He knew they weren't far from the Nassau County line but couldn't recall which was the easternmost bridge. The woman found what she wanted, a rapid-fire disk jockey, and turned up the volume, grimly satisfied, her look directed toward the top of the stairs.

Marina was squat, close to shapeless, dressed in what might have been thrift-shop clothing. Her face had precise lines, however, strongly boned, a trace of the socialist painter's peasant woman, broad arcs and shadows. Her hair was parted in the middle and combed back over the ears. She had eyes that concentrated intently and would not easily surrender their assertiveness. She believed in one thing, he felt, to the exclusion of everything else. Although he didn't know what this thing was as yet, he was certain she'd imbued it with a particular kind of purity, a savage light.

"You didn't meet my brother, unfortunately. Only Rosemary, is that right? My brother did the rockets at Tempelhof. He planned it to the last detail."

"I don't know if I recall."

"They hit the wrong plane. They hit the DC-9. They were totally stupid. One plans something to the closest degree of precision. What happens?"

"They go and hit the wrong plane," he said.

The place was full of blond furniture, secondhand, the kind of thing found in rec rooms or settlement houses. Everything had a chemical veneer. Marina put the groceries away and made some phone calls, not bothering to reduce the volume on the radio. During the third such call, J. Kinnear came down the stairs, moving quickly, feet wide apart, taking the last few steps with a rhythmic little canter. Five nine or ten, Lyle thought, identifying yet another suspect for some detective lieutenant. Checked shirt, brown pants, brown loafers, older than he appeared to be at very first glance.

"Hi, I'm J. Delighted. You want to turn, is that it?"

He smiled, shaking Lyle's hand, half winking, and sat on a stack of phone books, hunched forward, clutching his knees. His manner suggested they were fellow believers whose paths had diverged only through the force of horrid circumstance. Furthermore he was eager to hear the whole story. There was humor in the way Kinnear assembled this sense of flattering intimacy. He was at a distance from it but certainly not in a way intended to deceive. His hands were at his ankles now, absently scratching. Marina turned off the radio and made another phone call. The room hummed as the two men waited for her to speak before resuming their own conversation. Kinnear had a gaze that never quite penetrated. If there was such a thing as being stared at evasively, Lyle felt he was experiencing just that. Rusty brown hair. Remnants of widespread freckling. Creases about the eyes and mouth.

"A man from the floor itself."

"The floor of floors."

"Delighted, delighted."

"What happens now?"

Kinnear laughed. He said he'd been making trips to and from the Coast. He said things were getting interesting. Lyle

inferred that he wasn't supposed to ask questions. The room
was warm. He wanted to go to sleep. He couldn't understand
why he wasn't more alert, more interested. From the beginning, when Marina Vilar picked him up outside a bookstore
on Fourth Avenue and took a less than direct route to the
Midtown Tunnel, Lyle hadn't been able to feel wholly en-
gaged. It was happening around him somehow. He was slipping right through. A play. It was a little like that. He found
himself bored, often, at the theater (although never at movies), even when he knew, could see and hear, that the play
was exceptional, deserving of total attention. This kind of tor-
por was generated by three-dimensional bodies, real space as
opposed to the manipulated depth of film. So things here
might take a while to pinch in, raise a welt or two. In the
meantime she'd taken him shopping. He'd followed her up and
down the aisles of a small market in Bayside.

"What's curious," he said to Kinnear, "is the little sort of
reversal here. I'm a white collar. A walk-in. That was the
secret dream of the white collar. To place a call from a public
booth in the middle of the night. Calling some government
bureau, some official department, right, of the government.
'I have information about so-and-so.' Or, even better, to be
visited, to have them come to you. 'You might be able to
deliver a microdot letter, sir, on your visit to wherever,' if
that's how they do things. 'You might be willing to provide a
recruiter with cover on your payroll, sir.' Imagine how sexy
that can be for the true-blue businessman or professor. What
an incredible nighttime thrill. The appeal of mazes and intricate techniques. The suggestion of a double life. 'Fantastic,
sign me up, I'll do it.' 'Of course, sir, you won't be able to tell

anyone about this, including your nearest and dearest.' 'I love it, I love it, I'll sign.' But what's happening *here*, J.? That's the twist. You have somebody like George Sedbauer, to name just one instance of what I'm talking about, and what was old George up to, a white collar like old George? He was hanging around with the wild-eyed radicals, with the bomb-throwers. He was doing business with the other side. A white collar. What happened to the bureau, the service, the agency?"

Kinnear's smile emptied out as Lyle went along. The piano music stopped. He didn't change expressions; merely vacated his smile, leaving ridged skin behind. The woman passed between them and went upstairs. There was a pause. They waited for the effects of her presence to diminish, the simple distraction of her body in transit.

"Our phone bill is unreal. And we don't have two dimes to rub together."

"But somebody like Sedbauer involved with terrorists, these total crazies from the straight world's point of view. What does that suggest to you, J.?"

"I want to show you something. It'll be your initiation into the maze you spoke of. I have this fool notion that once you see this stuff, you're in for good. This nearly mystical notion."

Kinnear led the way to the basement. There was a door beyond the furnace. He snapped back the bolt and went into the back room. Lyle watched him lift paint-stained canvas from a large table. There was a stock of weapons on and under the table. Kinnear brushed dust from his hands, holding them out away from the rest of his body.

"I don't know how many rounds of machine gun ammunition."

He worked on his trouser legs now, concentrating on removing dust, and then, beginning to speak, turned to face Lyle across the table.

"Ironically no machine guns at the moment. But the usual sawed-off shotguns, sporting rifles, handguns. Some flak jackets. Some riot batons, riot helmets. Explosives and explosive components of various kinds, i.e., Pento-Mex, ammonium nitrate, various other powders and compounds. Ah, yes, an alarm clock for guess what purpose. Silhouette targets, cartridge clips, tracer bullets, a whole bunch of nine-volt batteries. I don't know how many cans of Mace and CN."

From that point, in sparse light, he seemed to be inviting a question or two, his head cocked and an element of serious expectation in his stance, generally—a fixing of distances. His hands were jammed into slash pockets, thumbs showing.

"Shouldn't this stuff be concealed better?"

"There's no reason for anyone to suspect this house of being anything out of the ordinary."

"Somebody comes down to fix the furnace."

"I come with him."

"And you're showing this stuff very freely, aren't you? What do you know about me, J.?"

"That's what she would say. Or her brother. But I operate on basic, really visceral levels. Terror is purification. When you set out to rid a society of repressive elements, you immediately become a target yourself, for all sorts of people. There's nobody who mightn't conceivably stick it to you. Being killed, or betrayed, sometimes seems the point of it all. As for what I know about you, Lyle, I would say you're George Sedbauer's successor. That's clear to me. This difference: George didn't know who he was working for. George thought we were involved in high-level—quote—industrial espionage—close quote. We led him to believe we represented international banking and shipping interests. He copied all sorts of arcane documents from his company's safes and files and told us whatever he knew about the Exchange itself. He thought Vilar was liaison man for some secret banking cartel. It never occurred to him until the end, literally the last minute, I would think, that Vilar wanted to blow up the Exchange."

"Boom."

"Vilar was a little bomb-happy for my taste. But there it is. And George in the meantime was wearing out the Xerox."

"Not knowing."

"I liked George. We got along. George was an interesting man. We spent time together."

"What did you do with the material he copied?"

"It was worthless."

"A lot of waxy paper."

"Look at this stuff," Kinnear said. "Riot shields, tear gas, all that anti-crowd business in the sixties. These are artifacts. This stuff is memorabilia. Aside from the explosives, I don't think any of this stuff even works anymore. And I can't really vouch for the explosives. Maybe these chemicals have an effective half life that expired ten minutes ago. But look at it all. Obviously hauled out of some National Guard armory in the middle of a night in spring. Pure nostalgia, Lyle. But I wanted you to see it. I would imagine a collection of weapons might have complex emotional content for someone in your position. It's an arsenal, after all. Only fair you know the nature of the game."

He propped one of the silhouette targets against the wall. He took out his handkerchief and cleaned off the top of an upended milk crate, then sat facing the target. He touched a finger several times to the dust on the face of the target. Entertainment, Lyle thought. A little show biz.

"It's this uncertainty over sources and ultimate goals," Kinnear said. "It's everywhere, isn't it? Mazes, you're correct. Intricate techniques. Our big problem in the past, as a nation, was that we didn't give our government credit for being the totally entangling force that it was. They were even more evil than we'd imagined. More evil and much more interesting. Assassination, blackmail, torture, enormous improbable intrigues. All these convolutions and relationships. Assorted sexual episodes. Terribly, terribly interesting, all of it. Cameras, microphones, so forth. We thought they bombed villages, killed children, for the sake of technology, so it could shake itself out, and for certain abstractions. We didn't give them credit for the rest of it. Behind every stark fact we encounter layers of ambiguity. This is all so alien to the liberal spirit. It's a wonder they're bearing up at all. This haze of conspiracies and multiple interpretations. So much for the great instructing vision of the federal government."

He turned from the target to face Lyle, who stood on the other side of the table.

"What really happened?" Kinnear said. "Who ordered the wiretaps? Why were the papers shredded and what did they say? Why does this autopsy report differ from that one? Was it one bullet or more? Who erased the tapes? Was so-and-so's death an accident or murder? How did organized crime get involved—who let *them* in? How deeply are the corporations involved in this or that mystery, this or that crime, these murders, these programs of systematic torture? Who ordered these massive surveillance programs? Who wrote the anonymous letters? Why did these witnesses drop out of sight? Where are the files? Where are the missing bullet fragments? Did this suspect work for the intelligence service or didn't he? Why do these four eyewitness accounts clash so totally? What happened, Lyle, on the floor that day?"

"I thought I'd get around to asking you."

"I wasn't there," J. said. "You were there. I didn't even know it was supposed to happen. They did it on their own. A brother-sister act."

"You want to know what happened."

"What happened, Lyle? How many shots were fired? Who did the shooting? Was it one person or more? Did you see a gun? What did the suspect or suspects look like?"

Kinnear paused here, summoning forensic energy for the windup.

"When governments become too interesting, the end is in sight. Their fall is contained not in their transgressions, obviously, but in the material that flows from these breaches, one minute sinister and vicious, the next nearly laughable. Governments mustn't be that interesting. It unsettles the body politic. I almost want to say they had too much imagination. That's not quite it, though, is it?"

"Fantasies."

"They had too many fantasies. Right. But they were our fantasies, weren't they, ultimately? The whole assortment. Our leaders simply lived them out. Our elected representatives. It's fitting, then, no more than fitting, and we were stone blind not to guess at it. All we had to do was know our own dreams."

"You ought to take this lecture on tour," Lyle said. "They pay well."

"I sense you're enjoying this. You need this, don't you? A sense of structure. A logical basis for further exposition."

Lyle heard footsteps right over him. A door closed, causing slight vibrations. He picked up what he thought might be an M-16. It was heavier than he'd expected. He held it at belly level, bouncing it lightly in his hands. Through a small window high on the wall he could see beyond the latticework that skirted the back porch. Marina was unfolding a beach chair in half shade. The weapon made him uneasy. The simple feel of it contained the severity of its ends. G-g-g-gun, he thought. No doubting its authority. Down to the smallest spiral groove it was clearly a device cut and shaped to function with chill precision. Memory of a toy's coppery taste on his tongue. The thing was near perfect. It could kill a man before the color of its stock registered in his mind. He put it down, deciding Kinnear was homosexual.

Later he sat out back with Marina. He didn't know who anyone was, really, but it didn't seem odd that he was here. He could have napped in his chair, easily, one hand cupped above the grass. Marina was reading a newspaper. She kept chopping at it to keep it compact in the wind.

"I'd like to ask if I can."

"What?"

"Why, exactly, you chose the Exchange to hit? Or is that too obvious?"

"The fact of George."

"He gave you access."

"They get threats. They're aware. Guards every few feet.

But having someone on the floor. It was handed to us. We knew we would do something. Rafael wanted to disrupt their system, the idea of worldwide money. It's this *system* that we believe is their secret power. It all goes floating across that floor. Currents of invisible life. This is the center of their existence. The electronic system. The waves and charges. The green numbers on the board. This is what my brother calls their way of continuing on through rotting flesh, their closest taste of immortality. Not the bulk of all that money. The system itself, the current. That's Rafael. The doctor of philosophy approach to bombing. 'Financiers are more spiritually advanced than monks on an island.' Rafael. It was this secret of theirs that we wanted to destroy, this invisible power. It's all in that system, bip-bip-bip-bip, the flow of electric current that unites moneys, plural, from all over the world. Their greatest strength, no doubt of that."

"What did Kinnear think of this?"

"They have money. We have destruction. What?"

"J.—what did he think?"

She looked back at the newspaper. Lyle felt it was important to ask questions that would not disappoint her. He may have missed right there. Kinnear was standing in the window above them, a telephone in his hand.

"It would have appealed to him if he had known. Not the bombing of itself. The thinking behind it. He would have discussed, discussed, discussed. J. is all theory. He's waiting for the instruments of world repression to fall apart on their own. It will happen mystically in a pink light. The people will step in and that will be that. One way of betraying the revolution is to advance theories about it. We don't only make doctrines, my brother and I. We're here to destroy. When we did the dynamite in Brussels, the embassy, it was beautiful because we were technicians completing an operation. In and out. The cleanest piece of work imaginable. Theory is an effete diversion. Its purpose is to increase the self-esteem of the theorists. The only worthwhile doctrine is calculated madness."

"Impossible to anticipate."

"Is one permitted to say 'moneys'—the plural?"

"Absolutely," he said.

In the early evening she drove him to a subway station. He had a long conversation with himself, internal. One voice was Lyle as a former astronaut who'd walked on the surface of the moon. The other voice was Lyle as a woman, interviewing the astronaut in a TV studio. The astronaut persona spoke movingly of weightlessness as a poetic form of anxiety and isolation. Somewhere at the top of the original Lyle's head, the interviewer smiled and cleared her throat. They drove past houses, more houses. Then they were on Main Street, Flushing.

"Rosemary doesn't know me as Vilar. She knows me as Marina Ramirez."

"Okay, good."

"But you know me as Vilar."

"Correct."

The woman persona asked questions about colors and shapes, loneliness among the stars. Will we ever walk on Mars, she said. There were waits for lights to change. The conversation trailed off. He felt stupid, having had it. Marina was watching him as she glided to a stop behind a line of other cars.

"We still have the intent to hit Eleven Wall."

He didn't react.

"It has to be shattered to whatever extent we can manage before they decide to close it down for their own purposes. All this decentralization we see. It is a reaction to terror? I amuse myself by thinking they have a master plan to eliminate prominent targets. To go underground. Or totally electric. Nothing but waves and currents talking to each other. Spirits. So, the thing should be hit to whatever extent, now."

"Thus your interest in a second George."

"It's easier with a George."

"I would think so."

"Don't you think?"

"I would certainly think so."

"Of course a George isn't everything," she said. "We need a Vilar as well. Someone who does explosives in his sleep."

Lyle got out of the car, automatically checking his pockets for keys, change, wallet, cigarettes. He watched her edge away into light traffic. They'd changed to Ohio plates.

He spent the evening in the district. It was hazy and dense, even by the river. Two men ignored a third, their buddy, urinating, as they wrestled in slow motion near the tennis dome at the foot of Wall, one of them trying to reach a bottle the other had in his back pocket. Lyle turned a corner and walked slowly west. He knew the lack of activity was deceptive, time of day, day of week, an illusion of relief from the bash of predatory engineering. Inside some of the granite cubes, or a chromium tower here and there, people sorted money of various types, dizzying billions being propelled through machines, computer-scanned and coded, filed, cleared, wrapped and trucked, all in a high-speed din, that rip of sound intrinsic to deadline activities. He'd seen the encoding rooms, the microfilming of checks, money moving, shrinking as it moved, beginning to elude visualization, to pass from a paper existence to electronic sequences, its meaning increasingly complex, harder to name. It was condensation, the whole process, a paring away of money's accidental properties, of money's touch. Somehow he'd come back to South Street. All three men wrestled now, back-pedaling in a roistering circle that seemingly had the bottle at its center. Their grappling took place in even slower motion than it had before, a film of reaching and mistimed grips, and they murmured and cursed, hanging on. What remained, he thought, could hardly be identified as money (itself, in normal forms, a compression of one's worth). The process remained, Marina's waves and charges, a deathless presence. Lyle thought of his own money not as a medium of exchange but as something to be consigned to data storage, traceable only through magnetic flashes. Money was spiritual indemnity against some unspecifiable future loss. It existed in purest form in his mind, *my money,* a reinforcing source of meditation. He watched a woman move from phone to phone in a series of open booths outside an office building near the Cotton Exchange. This view of money, he felt, was not the healthiest. Secrecy, possessiveness, cancer-bearing rationality. The woman, depositing no coins, lifted the phone off the hook, screamed something into it, then threw it back into the booth. After she'd done this to the sixth and last phone, hurling it fiercely, she saw Lyle approach and smiled at him, her raw skin cracking. When he smiled back, blinking a bit, she said: "Suck out my asshole, mister." He stopped, watching her hobble down the street. Then he picked up one of the dangling phones and called Rosemary Moore, letting it ring and ring.

2

Pammy bare-breasted on the redwood deck watched Ethan row toward shore, varying light between them, fire opal and conifer bronze, a checkered shade from house to water's edge, curt blue noon beyond. She sat on a bench while Jack Laws cut her hair. The house was all glass and cedar shingles, built vertically, its reflecting surfaces dense with trees. Jack muttered instructions to himself, thinning out an area behind her left ear. She looked west toward silhouetted hills, the mainland.

"What are you up to back there?"

"You wanted drama, right? A change. Don't interrupt."

"What'll we do for lunch?"

"That's all we do here. We plan meals at great length with all this business about fresh vegetables, fresh lobster, country-fresh eggs, this bullshit routine. We talk about it, right? Then we actually plan it, the specifics. Then we do it, we make it. Then we sit down and eat it, talking about it all the while."

"I don't want you doing things to my hair in this mood."

"Then we, what, clean up, throw away, wash and dry. And then it's time to discuss mealtime, foodtime, the next meal. Quick, drive out to roadside stands. Blueberries, squash, corn, hurry."

"It's not a life-enhancing mood you're in. I sense little warmth there, Jack."

"After dark," he said. "The quiet."

"I don't like scissors in your hand."

"Do you believe how dark?"

"It's called night, Jack. We call that night."

"I didn't know it would be like this. I thought swimming at least. Do you believe this water?"

"Cold, I know."

"I thought morning swims. I thought at last, freedom from crowded beaches. But this water. Who knew?"

"It's not totally out of the question."

"It's the pits."

"Try again," she said. "Maybe it was just that day."

"You have nice breasts."

"A bit hairy right now."

"Nice breasts for a girl."

"I still want to know what we'll do for lunch."

"If he ever gets here to supervise."

"He rows well, I think."

"The supervisor," Jack said. "If the supervisor ever gets here."

"Anytime Ethan wants to rent a house this nice in a setting this lovely, cetra cetra, I'm perfectly happy to have him supervise."

"What's he got in that boat, four tons of pig iron, the way he's rowing?"

"I like watching him. People rowing. People rowing and people bicycling. They're nice to watch. Once we were in England and somewhere near Windsor Castle we saw these boys rowing, prep school, in racing boats, rowing as teams in these sculls, and along the shore there's the instructor going along on this little path right along the shore on his bicycle, this towpath, calling out instructions."

"I'm doing this par excellence."

"So rowing and bicycling together," she said. "Boy, what a treat for my jaded cranium."

"This is drama extraordinaire."

"All I want's a new head."

"You got it, charley."

She'd always lived in apartments. This was a house in the woods at the edge of a bay, a house that inhaled the weather, frequent changes in temperature. She heard noises all night long. Animals lived in the roof and cellar. There were bats in the unused chimney. In bed, curled under blankets and quilts, she couldn't tell the difference between the sounds of wind and rain, or bats and squirrels, or rain and bats. There were ship-creakings everywhere and charred wood hissing in the fire-place, sputtering up at times, never quite still. When fog worked in from the bay it seemed to suggest some basic change in the state of information. The dampness in foul weather was penetrating. Birds flew into the huge glass windows, seeing forest within, and were stunned or killed.

They watched Ethan step out of the dinghy and pull it onto the stony beach, up over the tide line. He came up the make-shift steps and along a bending path, disappearing in the trees once or twice, head down when he emerged, trudging. Pammy went inside to find a shirt.

3

Lyle watched television, sitting up close, his hand on the channel selector. Near midnight he got a call from J. Kinnear. He imagined Kinnear looking out the window as he spoke, down at the dark yard.

"Where will you be Tuesday, eleven-thirty, night?"

"Happening fast."

"If I were an intelligence officer putting you through a prerecruitment phase, I'd be inclined to move very slowly. I'd be inclined, I think, to let you discover your limit of involvement at a much more reasonable pace."

"How far I'd go."

"Correct."

"My clandestine potential."

"Be at night court, Centre Street. I may want you to meet someone."

"Any idea how I can reach Rosemary?"

"None," J. said.

Two days later, after the close, he saw the green VW turn into Wall from Broadway. Marina pulled over and he got in. She drove out to the gray frame house. Kinnear was sitting out back, legs crossed, writing on a legal pad. From the small porch Lyle looked back in for Marina, seeing her through a series of doorways as she passed the entrance to the basement, near the front of the house, apparently talking to someone. Kinnear approached Lyle, gripping his upper arm as they shook hands and flashing that quick wink, an expression that said "trust, solidarity, purpose."

"Lyle in his work duds."

"Best tie too."

"Big-time trading duds."

"She forgot the Cheerios."

Memory stirring in J.'s eyes.

"Yes—yes, she did, matter of fact. The Cheerios. Ruined two breakfasts."

J. went back to his chair, his right hand trailing a sense of their recent handshake, and Lyle sat on the porch steps.

"How are you?"

"There's a feeling we've been penetrated. Consequently a certain amount of disinformation is being handed out. It gets a little complex at times."

"Disinformation is what?"

"A term used by intelligence agencies. Meaning's clear enough, no?"

"Plausible but erroneous information."

"So," Kinnear said, "there's a slight taste of cat piss in the air. Ambiguity, confusion, disinformation. What next, right?"

"Do you head up this group or whatever?"

"I don't confirm, I don't deny. Yes and no, but don't quote me on that. I'm a little bit of a Jesuit, Lyle. Jebbies know how to play position. They don't leave you with a good shot."

"You weren't told of the first attempt."

"Yes, well, the brother-sister act comes to us with a fair measure of self-righteous zeal attached to it. But that's all right, perfectly all right. We don't have a prospectus and we don't put out an annual report. Any rate, I wasn't supposed to tell you about the penetration. But I want your trust, Lyle. I may be needing it, frankly. I've been living in pavement cracks for a number of years now and you get so you trust the near stranger or at least go out of your way to vie for his trust because that's one of the things that happens. You get some complicated feelings about your own people. When somebody's picked up, wow, you can't imagine how quick you are to forget all that clan solidarity you've been building for years. It's assumed he or she will furnish names and places. Things change and maybe it's advanced communications, I don't know, but today there's just one terrorist network and one police apparatus. Thing is, they sometimes overlap."

Kinnear walked over to the steps and put his hands to Lyle's face, framing it. He recited a phone number, speaking with exaggerated distinctness. He asked Lyle to memorize the number and instructed him to use it only at his, J.'s, specific request. Then he went back to the chair, openly venting his apprehensions in a pasty smile. He was vulnerable in the special way of men who still inhabit the physical structure and display the mannerisms of their early twenties, a relatively blameless age. J. had no less trouble being slender these days, or light afoot, and there were signs, still, of an ingenuous eager warmth in his eyes. This honesty was cruel, however, a suggestion of some essential deficiency in the man, his failure to understand deception, perhaps, or anything besides deception.

"Somebody like Vilar," Lyle said, "would be an example, I take it, of one network."

This was the evening he was supposed to show up at night court to meet Kinnear's friend or associate or contact. He thought it would be "professional" not to mention it unless J. did.

"Vilar—good example. A man, the story goes, who's

wanted in x number of countries. Linked, as they say, with separatist groups here, with exiles there, with nationalists, guerrillas, extremists, leftist death squads, whatever they are. I hope for his own sake the man isn't double-celled. A mite touchy and high-strung."

"What about somebody like George? I speak as a George myself. How exactly did George get involved?"

"How George got involved was this. We were using Rosemary as a courier. She was flying then, New York to San Francisco and New York–Munich, I think. It's safer and obviously cheaper to use crew instead of regular travelers. Anyway she and George Sedbauer met somewhere and he gradually became part of things, more or less. I wouldn't say she recruited him. It wasn't that carefully diagrammed. He told her he was in debt. She brought him to us. We promised him money, which we never delivered on and which he made only halfhearted requests for. I guess he enjoyed all that photocopying."

"But drew the line at bombs."

"George is paged," Kinnear said. "He goes out to the desk and sees Vilar. Things are kind of quiet today so George picks up a guest badge, which Vilar slips over his breast pocket, and they walk past the security guards and onto the floor of the Exchange. There's a conversation. George gets suspicious. What is this guy telling me? They talk some more. It dawns on George. This guy wants to leave explosives, a battery and a timing device in some fairly central part of the Exchange. Vilar hasn't told him this in so many words. But George is on to it; he knows, finally. There's no question but that he'll abort the attempt. Next thing, he's walking away from Vilar, who goes after him. There's a struggle. Vilar takes out a gun and fires, hitting George once in the lungs. Or is it twice?"

"Good question."

"Or," Kinnear said, "George had two visitors on the floor that day. There was a second gunman. It was a bullet or bullets from this second man's gun that killed George. Not only that but he made it to the street. If I recall, early reports mentioned a chase through the streets."

"True."

"And for quite a while the police had trouble identifying the killer."

"Equally true."

"The second gunman was Luis Ramirez. He not only made it to the street; he escaped clean. Who is Ramirez, exactly? Let's say he's a rather obscure figure who's spent time in the Middle East and Argentina, presumably assisting the local movements and maybe picking up some handy bits of know-how. An exchange program, let's say. Known heretofore as an expert in falsifying passports. He's also Vilar's brother-in-law. An investigation will reveal the usual police inefficiency. It will show, specifically, that the bullet that killed George came from a seven point six-five millimeter Mauser automatic, not some starter's pistol, which is what they found at the scene."

Kinnear crossed out a line or two on the pad before him. Lyle wanted a cold drink. He'd had a craving for something cold to drink since leaving the Exchange. Kinnear crossed out something else, this time with a little flourish of his ballpoint pen.

"Or," he said, "George ambles onto the floor. In one of his pockets is a miniature explosive device that includes detonator and receiving set. He has acquired it with the help and encouragement of his lover, Marina Ramirez, and it's no larger, really, then a ten-blade dispenser. The plan is simple. Leave the device in a message slot in one of the booths. Stroll casually out the front door of Eleven Wall. Get into the waiting Volkswagen. Drive, with Marina, to a point about half a mile away. Activate the device with a radio signal sent from a transmitter in the car. Explosion, death, chaos. What actually happens is George is followed onto the floor by Rafael Vilar, a man George has met at various places maybe half a dozen times, a sort of fringe figure, last seen at Lake Placid, where he spent a whole weekend panting after Rosemary Moore. Turns out Vilar is a police operative. Or, better, an extremist who turned. Naturally he aborts the attempt. The rest you know, more or less. A struggle. A shot or two. George dead. Vilar hauled into custody, temporarily, in an effort to safeguard the integrity of his role, prior to his retirement north of the border. Admittedly the weakest scenario. George's motive, for one thing, is unknown. We have to assume Marina was the activating force. Passion for Marina, et cetera, made him willing to comply. He'd been passed on, you see, from Rosemary to Marina. Sort of a promotion, with all the attendant responsibilities and risks."

"Does Luis Ramirez exist in this scenario?"

"Doesn't enter into it, no. But I wouldn't say he doesn't exist."

"Is Marina married to him?"

"Could be; I don't know."

"Is she related to Vilar?"

"Absolutely not."

"In this scenario."

"Or," Kinnear said, "Vilar in his revolutionary fervor decides it's time for the ultimate gesture. He will give his life for the cause. Perfectly in keeping. Vilar has always had tendencies. The rightist kills his own leader. The leftist kills himself. Taking as many people with him as can be accommodated in a given area. In this case a superb sadomasochistic coup. Half the Exchange goes with him. This, in its surface aspects, is scenario one, minus the timing device. George aborts, et cetera."

"I think there has to be a reason besides revolutionary fervor why he'd commit suicide."

"Check with Marina on that."

"Did the bomb they found on Vilar really have a timing device?"

"No idea," Kinnear said.

"The papers must have said. I don't recall, though."

"Don't ask me, Lyle. You were there."

"I was there, correct."

"In your well-pressed suit."

Marina took him to a different train this time. She wore baggy clothes, smeared with paint and varnish. He watched her extract a crushed cigarette from the pack in her trouser pocket, leaning far to one side as she drove through heavy traffic. Vengeance, he thought. She would be the type who dedicated herself to exacting satisfaction for some wrong. She would work on personal levels, despite the sweeping references to movements and systems. It was possibly at the center of her life, the will to settle things, starkly. Coercive passions sometimes had a steadying element in their midst. To avenge, in a sense, was simply to equalize, to seek a requisite balance. There was forethought involved, precision of scale. Lyle watched her put a match to the bent cigarette. He'd never felt so *intelligent* before. His involvement was beginning to elicit an acute response. They had no visible organization or leadership. They had no apparent plan. They came from nowhere and might be gone tomorrow. Lyle believed it was these free-form currents that he found so stimulating, mentally. They gave no indication of membership in anything. They didn't even have a nationality, really.

She parked near the station.

"What did J. tell you?"

"There's been a penetration."

"We believe."

"Yes, a feeling, he said."

"Do you know he colors his hair?"

"I love it."

"It's the kind where the color changes gradually, a little a day. Then you touch up."

"Comb your gray away."

"He used to be a counselor," she said. "What do you know about that?"

"Nothing."

"He used to be a counselor with a group up in the mountains somewhere, out west. Group sessions."

"Encounter."

"Encounter," she said. "It was clearly the thing. He conducted sessions. They all found God, et cetera."

"That's where He lives, you know, in the mountains."

"What can you add to this?"

"Nothing," he said.

"Nothing about a kidnapping? About when he was involved with a group in New Orleans?"

"No."

"But he told you what we discussed."

"Disinformation."

"If you get a phone call and hear my voice, and if I stumble and mutter and tell you that I think I've dialed the wrong number, and if I then say the number I intended to get, write down and memorize the first, third, fourth, fifth and seventh digits. You'll be hearing again eventually."

"First, third, fourth, fifth and seventh."

"The rest is padding," she said.

Later he went to Centre Street. Night court consisted of policemen in and out of uniform, occupying the front rows, and about sixty others, families of the accused and of victims, spread elsewhere. There was no judge at present. Lyle watched a legal aid lawyer, a young woman in a J. Edgar Hoover sweat shirt. She talked to people seated through the courtroom and to others clustered in the aisles, Kafkian lawyers, scavenging. A judge walked in and people began to assume various stances. As cases were heard, there was a general sense of men and women straining to understand what was going on—what forces, exactly, had caused this cruelty and ruin. A cop turned in his seat, yawning. It was well past the time Kinnear had mentioned. Lyle watched the woman conferring with three black men in a far corner of the room. They were in their twenties, one of them sitting in a wheelchair. Lyle waited half an hour longer, the voices around him sounding as though they'd been generated by machine, some regulator of flawed destinies.

At home he drank two glasses of ice water. He started to call McKechnie, despite the hour, when he remembered Frank's wife was ill, his oldest child was behaving strangely, there were problems, problems. He closed all the windows and turned on the air conditioner and the TV set in the bedroom. All the lights were out. He smoked, watching a film about glass blowing, with perky music, and tried to imagine what Kinnear was doing or saying at the moment, or what he'd do tomorrow, whom he'd call, where he'd go and how he'd get there. Kinnear was hard to fit into an imagined context. Lyle could not reposition him or invent types of companions or even the real color of his hair. He occupied a self-enfolding space, a special level of exclusion. Beyond what Lyle had seen and heard, Kinnear evaded a pattern of existence.

Lyle switched to a movie about a man suspected of embezzlement. The man's wife, a minor character, wore low-cut blouses. She had brightly painted lips and kept taking cigarettes out of a silver case and then tapping them against the top of the case, totally bored by her husband's crime. Out-of-date sexiness appealed to Lyle. He stayed with the movie, bad as it was, waiting for glimpses of the wife, her low-cut blouse. When the movie was over he began switching channels every ten or fifteen seconds, drinking Scotch. At three in the morning he called Pammy on Deer Isle.

"Ethan, it's Lyle."

"Good God, man."

"Don't tell me I woke you. I didn't wake you."

"I was reading."

"This is New York on the phone."

"By the fire," he said. "I was pretending to be reading by the fire."

"The city's in a state of incipient panic. Invasion of strange creatures. Objects are hovering in the air even as I speak."

"You don't know how unfunny that is."

"I think I do, actually."

"Jack claims he saw a UFO tonight. Naturally we were mildly skeptical. Well, this upset him. Jack's upset. Nobody believes his story."

"Wouldn't finish his veggies."

"Went to bed without his Calder penguin."

"Is she up?"

"I'll get her," Ethan said.

Lyle turned to watch the TV screen.

"So that was you," she said. "You like waking people up. How are you?"

"Having fun?"

"This place is so great. Of course I have to say that—he's five feet away. But it is, it's just great. Gets a little cold at night, I'd say. Yes, a little nippy. Like I'm freezing to death. But we're coping well. How are you?"

"The city's in a state of incipient panic."

"I don't want to hear about it."

"So what it's like, trees?"

"We went to this terrific place today. Weaving, they did weaving, quilting, pottery. The whole schmeer, you know? I'm pretending to like it—he's five feet away. No, seriously, did you ever see how glass is blown?"

"No, tell me."

"So, okay, it's a little boring. No, it's not, I'm teasing Ethan. Listen, I'll wake up Jack. If he's still here. You can talk to him. If he hasn't been spirited away in a little green capsule."

"I heard."

"We'll make an event out of it. I'll get Jack."

They talked a while longer. She didn't get Jack. After he hung up he watched television. As time passed it became more difficult for him to turn off the set. He knew an immense depression would settle in between the time he turned off the set and the time he finally fell asleep. He would have to resume. That's why it was so hard to turn off the set. There would be a period of resuming. He wouldn't be able to go to sleep immediately. There would be a gap to fill. It caused a tremendous wrench, turning off the set. He was *there,* part of the imploding light. The room he occupied was unfamiliar for a moment. He had to learn it all over again. But it wasn't as bad as he'd expected. Only a routine depression settled in and he was asleep within the hour.

4

Rosemary was at her desk, sorting mail. These surroundings no longer made sense. He'd seen her in a half slip, in panties, naked. He'd stood in the toilet doorway and watched her dress, an itemizing of erotic truths, until she'd spotted him and turned, off-balance, to elbow the door. At her desk, passing time, he marveled at the ease with which they fitted into slots of decorum. People must be natural spies. The desk, the broadloom were absurd. Her letter opener, neatly slitting. His tone of voice.

He waited for her after work in front of her house. They went inside and drank for several hours. He held her hand, occasionally putting his lips to the ends of her fingers. He realized this was an endearment.

In the kitchen he took another look at the picture of her with Sedbauer and Vilar. He studied Vilar's face. It was shiny and lean, a high forehead, tapered jaw. He heard her in the bedroom, Rosemary's clothes coming off.

Curled into herself she waited, an animal void, white body, deep stillness, the thing he tried to hand-grip and eat. He wouldn't urge her toward some vast shuddering fuck or recollect the touch of her hands at the end of a passive afternoon, some months off, paper sailing as his soul wandered from the floor. She extended her limbs. He could see breasts now, her face and neck, her arms and small hands, half cupped, and the wrinkled sheet between her thighs. He'd never before seen how different a woman's body was from his own. This fact, somehow, had been hidden from him. Am I drunk, he wondered. Supine she seemed enormous, nearly outsizing the small bed. That was good, that was right, deep stillness, organic void. Her breathing caused a perceptible cadence, body's periodic rise and fall, a metronome of his calculated lust. Slightly misshapen feet. Small bumps, flesh points, at the rims of her nipples. He undressed slowly, knowing neither of them would reach an interval of fulfilling labor, or whistle a bit, breathing nasally, and cry a name, all perspective burnt from their faces. She touched her ribs where a fly had landed. This automatic motion revealed her, briefly. In a haze he understood at last. But what? Understood, at last, what? The fly settled on a window sill. He watched it, trying to retrace its connection to the huge body on the bed, the bone and muscle structure of a dream. There were pale veins on her legs, sun lines and natural indentations. Knees up, head way back over the curve of the pillow, she might have been half yielding to, half defending against, some clumsy lover. He crawled, literally crawled between her legs. Then he rested his forearms on her raised knees and watched the way her throat lightly pulsed.

"Tell me some more about George," he said. "What did he do besides make you laugh?"

He crossed the street to the candy store tucked in at 77 Water, red and yellow awning, a homey footnote to the mass of steel and anodized aluminum. There was gray everywhere, wetness suspended, a day the color of the district itself. He bought cigarettes and chewing gum and then stood outside the candy store, under the bulk of the skyscraper, and unwrapped a stick of gum, listening for foghorns, a sound he associated with foreign cities and sex with other men's wives. It didn't take him long to realize he was being stared at. Man near the entrance to the lobby. Checked sportcoat, solid tie. Lyle had the impression the man wanted him to walk that way. He was stocky and boyish, a frozen jaw, wisps of hair curled down over his forehead. Lyle decided to go in the other direction. About two blocks away the man came alongside. Lyle stopped, waiting for a light to change. The man looked at him again, clearly intent on conveying some tacit information, a connection or message he expected Lyle to perceive. They walked another half block. Two women up ahead raised umbrellas simultaneously.

"You're McKechnie's friend, aren't you?"

"Is life that simple?" the man said.

"I kept waiting for you people to contact me. I talked to Frank McKechnie about the situation. About what certain people knew. Frank talked to someone to pass the word along. I expected earlier contact. In the meantime I decided to find out what I could."

"That was outstanding, Lyle."

"What's your name?"

"Burks."

"Burks, your tone of voice isn't encouraging."

"We do what we can."

"They have contacts on the West Coast. I know that. They use Ohio plates, at least at the moment. I know the number if you want it. A green Volkswagen, or do you have all this?"

"What can you tell us about A. J. Kinnear?"

"It's J. Kinnear at present."

"We have A. J."

"It's just J. now."

"Just J.," Burks said.

"I don't know how many people are involved. If they have units or teams or whatever, I couldn't tell you how they're set up. Kinnear is a complex individual, I think. They're out in Queens. I know the street name and house number."

"Is Kinnear tall, short, what?"

They walked up and down the streets near the river. Lyle described Kinnear, speaking slowly and then listening with care, trying to memorize his own remarks and what Burks said in reply. It was like a conversation with a doctor who was reporting the results of significant tests. Questions and answers floated through each other. One's life seemed to hinge on syntax, inflection, points of grammar. He thought Burks said something about a voiceprint but wasn't sure of the context, whether it applied to Kinnear or not. It was also a little like his early conversations with Rosemary Moore, photographs of his own mouth, the sense of her remarks eluding him not only as they were uttered but later as well, in his attempts to narrate to himself the particulars of each encounter. He saw a barge in the haze, perhaps midriver, sliding toward the harbor. Burks' shoes gleamed. He was young, probably younger than Lyle.

"They may take another crack at the Exchange."

"We'd be interested."

"What else?"

"What else—what do you mean?"

"Is there anything else you want to know?" Lyle said. "They have a basement full of retread weapons. I can describe them if you want. I have this annoying faculty."

"What's that?"

"Compulsive information-gathering."

"It must be a burden."

"Tone of voice," Lyle said.

"Fuck you, cookie."

"Are you McKechnie's friend or not?"

"You talked to Frank McKechnie. He said he'd talk to a friend of his. If you want to believe my presence here is a direct result of McKechnie's communication, feel free, Lyle. But there's a question I'd like to pose."

"What's that?"

"Is life ever that simple?"

"Nice."

"We do what we can."

"No, nice, really, I like it."

"Good, Lyle."

"What can you tell me about Vilar?"

"I can tell you to eat shit off a wooden stick," Burks said.

Just another Fordham or Marquette lad. Studied languages and history. Played intramural sports. Revered the Jesuits for their sophistication and analytical skills. Voted for moderates of either party. Knows how to strangle a German shepherd with rosary beads.

Lyle walked crosstown to busier areas. It was getting dark. He moved to one side to avoid some people stepping off a bus. One of them made momentary contact, putting an arm out to ward off a collision, a man with a mustache and wiry hair, muttering something, his head large and squarish. Keep yer distance, mon. Lyle looked around for a public phone as he walked on. It started raining hard and the streets gradually emptied out. Don't be settin' yer hands on honest folk. He found a bar, ordered a drink and went back to the phone booth. One of McKechnie's daughters answered, saying she'd get her father.

"That friend of yours."

"What about him?"

"Burks," Lyle said. "Is that his name?"

"No."

"Call him up, Frank, and find out if he knows who Burks is."

"I made my call."

"You can do that."

"I made my call. That was it."

"Call him. I'll get right back to you."

"Sure, get right back."

"I'll call you in fifteen minutes."

"Sure, call, Lyle, anytime."

He went to the bar and sipped his drink. A man with crutches stood nearby, a near derelict, it seemed. It wasn't much of a place. Two elderly women sat at a far corner of the bar, sharing a cigarette. Lyle finished his drink. It was too soon to call McKechnie again. He ordered another Scotch and went back to phone J. Kinnear, realizing, with profound surprise, that he didn't know how to get in touch with Kinnear. The listing would be in another name, obviously, and Lyle had never thought to check the number on the telephone in the frame house in Queens. Dumb, very dumb. When he got back to the bar he saw someone walk past the front door, hurrying through the rain, a man holding a newspaper over his head. Just a glimpse was all. Wee glimpse o' the laddie's mustache. A little later a woman came in and greeted the man on crutches, asking what had happened.

"I got runned over by a learner driver."

"Did you sue his ass?"

"What sue?" he said. "I was like on the brink."

"You could collect, Mikey. People do it. You could make a nice little something for yourself."

"I was like seeing cherubs."

Or an M.A. in economics, he thought. Big Ten fencing titles. Square head, wiry hair. Author of a study on trade regulations in Eastern Europe. Does push-ups with his knuckles.

Lyle walked down Nassau Street. The district was a locked sector. Through wavering layers of rain he saw it that way for the first time. It was sealed off from the rest of the city, as the city itself had been planned to conceal what lay around it, the rough country's assent to unceremonious decay. The district grew repeatedly inward, more secret, an occult theology of money, extending ever deeper into its own veined marble. Unit managers accrued and stockpiled. Engineers shampooed the vaults. At the inmost crypt might be heard the amplitude pulse of history, a system and rite to outshadow the evidence of men's senses. He stepped out of a doorway and hailed the first free cab he saw, feeling intelligent again.

At home he heard from Kinnear almost immediately. He stood holding the phone, concentrating intently, determined to understand what was being said, the implications, the shadings, whatever petalous subtleties might be contained in the modulations of J.'s voice.

"I'm not where I usually am."

"Right."

"I'll be sort of transient—I would say indefinitely."

"Before that, there's something that happened. I talked to a Burks, if you know the name. He asked about you."

"Not unsurprisingly."

"Do you know who he is?"

"I may have talked to him on the phone. I talked to several of them. I wasn't given names. I had a number to call. We did our talking exclusively over the phone."

"I told him everything I know."

"That was clever, Lyle, actually."

"I thought I should tell you."

"I'm one of those people you've read about who's constantly being described as 'dropping out of sight,' or 'resurfacing.' As in: 'He resurfaced in Bogotá four years later.' Right now it's the former condition that prevails."

Lyle tried to imagine Kinnear in some specific locale, an airport (but there was no background of amplified voices) or remote house (where, what room) in a well-defined landscape. But he remained a voice, no more, a vibratory hum, coming from nowhere in particular.

"I asked him about Vilar," Lyle said. "He outright refused to tell me anything."

"Makes sense."

"They don't like me."

"Well, I talked to them, you know. We had talks about this and that."

"My name came up."

"I was very selective. That was part of the appeal of the whole experiment, from my viewpoint. It was interesting, very much so. I told them only certain things. They're quite a group—quite, let's say, adaptable, I guess is the word."

"They know my recent history."

"They know your recent history."

"And they didn't contact me earlier because they had someone inside."

"Now that I've severed all connections, Lyle, they've become very interested in you. You're their remaining means of tying into the little terror seminar."

"Can't they just go in and seize weapons and arrest people for that, if nothing else?"

"They'll find nothing there *but* weapons. I was the only person who spent any appreciable time in that house. Won't be anybody there, now or later."

"I thought Marina."

"Marina was out there maybe half a dozen times, never for longer than a couple of hours."

"Why pick now to travel, J.?"

"I was getting bricked in, old man. The element you think of in the person of Marina was clearly aware that information was trickling. The element you think of in the person of Burks was getting a touch possessive. It was time to do a one-eighty out the door."

Lyle suspected J. was getting ready to hang up.

"How long have you been giving information?"

"Matter of a few months."

"Get paid?"

"That was to come, eventually. Extremely doubtful I'll ever see it."

"Fair amount, I assume."

"Pittance."

"Why all the risk then?"

"People make experiments, Lyle. They're very adept at certain things, so aware of shadings, our secret police. I wanted to get inside that particular apparatus, just a step or two."

"They got your name slightly wrong."

"I didn't know they had it at all. That's interesting. See what I mean? Techniques. I wonder how they managed it. They must have spent a great deal of time on me. I used to wonder about that. Are they really interested in what they're getting? Do they know who I am? Their secrets are worse than ours, by far, which goes a long way toward explaining why their techniques are so well developed."

"What happens now?"

"I continue to ask for your trust."

"Don't go just yet, J."

"God bless," he said.

Lyle put down the phone, then dialed McKechnie's number. The little girl said her daddy didn't want to talk to him.

5

They discussed the sunset awhile, sitting on the deck with junk food and drinks. It was better than the previous day's sunset but lacked the faint mauve tones, according to Ethan, of the day before yesterday. They went inside and ate dinner, slowly, an uncoordinated effort. Jack complained that they were talking about the food while eating it, that they talked about sunsets while looking at them, so on, so forth. It was beginning to get on his nerves, he said. He used his semihysterical voice, that exaggerated whine of urban discontent. They sat by the fire after dinner, looking at magazines. Jack found a six-month-old *New York Times*. He read aloud from a list of restaurants cited for health code violations, chanting the names and addresses.

"We need wood," Ethan said.

"Wood."

"Bring in wood."

"Wood," Jack said.

"In bring," Pammy said. "Put pile."

"Wood, wood."

"Fire come," she said. "Make big for heat the body."

In the morning they drove over the causeway, their hair flattening in the wind, and then across the bridge to the mainland. The sky was everywhere. Pammy sat behind the men, smiling at the backs of their heads. Weathering had given the houses a second, deeper life, more private, a beauty that was skillfully spare, that had been won. Boulders in brown fields. The kids here, on bikes, barefoot. She scanned carefully for traces of water, eager to be surprised by it, to have it come up suddenly, an avenue of hard blue between stands of pine, sunlight bouncing on the surface. The kids on bikes were lean and blond, a little less than well-fed, a certain edge, she thought, to the way they returned her smile, looking hard at the car and the travelers, eyes narrow in the sun.

In Blue Hill they visited a married couple Ethan knew, three children, a dog. Leaving, she and Jack waited by the car while Ethan exchanged prolonged goodbyes with his friends. Jack was looking at her.

"I'm not really gay," he said.

"If you say so, Jack."

"I'm not, it's true."

"It's your mind and body."

"I should know, right?"

Late that afternoon she stepped out of the shower and felt pain, momentary pressure, at the side of her head. She would be dead within weeks. They'd force her to go through a series of horrible tests but the results would be the same every time. She was depressed, standing in a towel, her body slowly drying, dying. Waste, what a waste. She felt awful about Lyle. It would be easier for her to accept if she weren't leaving someone behind. Thank God no kids. She dressed and went outside.

After dinner they took the remaining wine and some brandy out to the deck. It was the mildest night they'd had. Jack was restless and decided to take the garbage over to the dump instead of waiting for morning. He got a flashlight and went up the path to the car, dragging two large plastic bags.

"He's right," Ethan said. "We can't seem to do anything without discussing it at the same time."

"Vacation," she said. "That's what people do."

"I hadn't realized we were doing it to the extent we were."

"Your German mouth is so serious."

"Maybe that's the secret meaning of new places."

"What is?"

"Quiet, I'm working it out."

"I don't want to hear."

"It concerns self-awareness," he said. "I'll give you the rest later."

"God, stars."

"The clearer everything is. That has something to do with it too."

"Look at them, millions."

"I am."

"Talk about them," she said. "Quick, before Jack comes back."

Much later there were long silences between periods of conversation. Jack brought out extra sweaters, then three blankets. When the wind rolled through the tops of trees, Pammy had trouble understanding the sound in its early stages, that building insistence of surf.

Later still, in some perfect interpenetration of wine and

night air, she drifted through a more congenial region, a non-space, really, in which immaculate calm prevailed. Between moments of near-sleep she felt her mind alive in the vivid chill. Clarity rang through every sparse remark. When Ethan laughed briefly, an idiot grunt, she felt she *knew* what tiny neural event had caused that sound. There was total order in the night.

Then she was sluggish and dumb. She wanted to be in bed but hadn't the will to get up and go inside. She kept edging into some unstable phase of sleep. Her elbow slipped off the inside of the chair arm, causing her to snap awake. Everything was different after that, a struggle.

"God, the stars," Jack said.

It occurred to Pam that Ethan rarely talked to Jack. He addressed Jack by talking about furniture, movies, the weather. That, plus third person. He said things to Pammy that were meant for Jack. Sometimes he read an item aloud from a newspaper or repeated a phrase spoken by a TV newsman, repeated it in a certain way—meant for Jack, some fragmentary parable. She didn't think this revealed as much about the two men involved as it did about people living together, their lesions of speech and demeanor. Pammy and Lyle had their own characteristics, of course. Pammy and Lyle, she thought. We sound like a pompom girl and a physics major. Or chimps, she thought. The names of chimps learning language with multicolored disks. She drank more wine, watching Ethan make a series of preliminary hand flourishes.

"New places, when they're really new, really fresh and new, make you more aware of yourself. This can be dangerous."

"I want my sleeping bag," Jack said.

"All this stuff is flashing your way. It's like a mirror, ultimately. You end up with yourself minus all the familiar out-
ward forms, the trappings and surroundings. If it's too new,
it's frightening. You get too much feedback that's not pre-
determined."

"Want sleep out," Jack said. "Air, wind."

"Fear is intense self-awareness."

"Like today, earlier," Pammy said, "when I thought I had
something wrong, I thought me, me, my tissue, my inner body.
But it's easier to die alone. Kids, forget about."

"Ground," Jack said. "Sleep, earth, creature."

Ethan ran the side of his index finger along his throat,
thoughtfully, and up over the point of his chin, many times—
an indication of ironic comments in the offing, or pseudo wis-
dom perhaps, or even autobiography, which, in his framework
of slanting planes, was itself determinedly ironic. They both
waited. It was the middle of the night. Water closed around
the rocks near shore, audibly, finding lanes.

"You people here."

Jack went inside, returning with a sleeping bag, which he
tossed on the deck. Everything was happening slowly now.
Jack went around lighting candles. Jack paced, imitating a
tiger. Pammy was aware that he was seated again, finally.
They drank awhile in silence.

"I'm slightly lantern-jawed," she said.

They seemed to laugh.

"No, really, people, I'm slightly lantern-jawed. It's all right.
It's, so what, no problem, long as I accept it."

"Pam-mee."

"So, you know, so what? When you think of other people's,

what they have to accept type thing. And it's slight, just hardly noticeable, I know that. So you accept. And you live. You simply everyday live."

"She's not about to blow her cookies, I hope."

"Your sleeping bag gets the brunt if I do."

"Mercy me."

"Blat," she said.

Pammy and Jack began a sequence of giddiness here. Everything was funny. She felt lightheaded, never more awake. Where was Ethan? She turned to see his profile, partly shrouded in the blanket, theatrical and grave. It would be dawn soon, maybe an hour or two, unfortunately at their backs somewhere. Jack's voice grew shrewd and dry. It was the only sound for a time. He paused between remarks, effectively. She laughed at everything he said. It was comical, this matter-of-fact Jack. She began to laugh at the end of pauses, anticipating. There was a spell of quiet. Softest color seeped into Pammy's awareness, something pared away from the night, a glow of the lowest resolution, as though night itself were being broken down into its optically active parts.

"You people here," Ethan said.

The others laughed.

"What you don't know is a whole era of things. You've been gone right by. It must be solid void to live without the references, although it's problematical that you even know it, this blank space. I mean a Pete Smith Specialty. Do you even imagine what this conjures up? No idea, have you? What it means when two people might meet, not knowing each other, and then to realize this association in their past, this small thing magnified, the utter dumbness of a Pete Smith Specialty, that narrator's voice, or tapes of Sin Killer Griffin recorded in some Texas jail. Hearing that's a footing of sorts, a solid footing. You missed that, see. Because, then, at that time, there wasn't this Zeitgeist of the Month business. It was all one thing, which you missed completely. *Pull My Daisy,* Jesus, which wasn't that long ago, with some of the people still around, but you don't know it, total nothing. *Pull My Daisy* at the Ninety-second Street Y. Or Lord Buckley, a whole thing you missed, Lord Buckley doing The Naz. No idea what I'm talking about, right? You missed the references. You missed the Village clubs. All the hanging around. The footing, the solid footing. You don't know, see, what you don't know is that your whole own attitudes come from some of these things, which were the basis, the solid rock. What else, who else can I mention? The Naz, I said that. Do you know how the Lone Ranger found Silver?"

Pammy became giddier. Jack arranged his sleeping bag across the length of a collapsible beach chair and got inside. Outlines of small islands became apparent. Ethan walked across the deck and opened the sliding door.

Later Jack struggled out of his sweater. A lobster boat appeared at the southern point of one of the islands. Pammy heard the first gull. There was an animal presence in the air, a binding of appetites.

It was slightly warmer now. She saw Jack's shirt on the deck. Things caught her eye continually, birds mostly, a small boat now and then, a seal close to shore, its slick head vanishing, reappearing. The binoculars were inside.

"All right, how many gay friends do I have?"

"What?" she said.

"Gay friends."

"How many does it take?"

"But you must have noticed how almost nobody I'm really friendly with is gay. Some, maybe, that I've lost touch with but Ethan thinks that are hanging around our building lobby and rooftop. Almost nobody by now."

"It only takes one, I thought."

"It's *my* mind and body," he said.

"Ah, point of agreement."

She forced herself to remove the blanket and get out of the chair, stiffly. She went inside, found the binoculars and came back out on the deck to look at the seal.

"I see myself doing a lot of traveling in the near future," Jack said. "Just place to place. An unsupervised existence. It's what I should have done a long time ago. I don't want to be pinned down anymore. Not in one place and not in one kind of life."

"He came up here because he thought it's what you wanted."

"He thought wrong."

"I think he's even prepared to make it more or less permanent, although how, financially, he expects to do this, I don't know."

"What are you looking at while I'm talking? I can't believe, Pam, I'm telling my life and you're with these binoculars, totally somewhere else."

"It's the seal, except it's gone, I think."

"The seal again, it's here?"

"The seal is back, except it's around that bend again, I think."

"Except it's not a seal," he said. "It's a frogman, spying."

She lay in bed, shivering a bit, curled away from the source of light. She tried to convince herself she was only seconds from sleep. Moments and episodes passed through her mind.

Later she woke up and heard Ethan in the kitchen, coughing noisily, bringing up phlegm and spitting it out. The bed was immersed in sunlight. She shed blankets, her body sprawling awake under a lone sheet, unbending to the comprehensive warmth.

For years she'd heard people saying, all sorts, really, here and there: "Do whatever you want as long as nobody gets hurt." They said: "As long as both parties agree, do it, whatever." They said: "Whatever feels right, as long as you both want to do it and nobody gets hurt, there's no reason not to." They said: "As long as there's mutual agreement and the right feeling, no matter who or what." "Whatever feels right," they said. They said: "Follow your instincts, be yourself, act out your fantasies."

6

Lyle hadn't been down here in years, the Lower East Side, that ethnic pantechnicon, *streets, people,* a history of flawless suffering. The car was parked on a side street near the Manhattan Bridge. Marina leaned forward, arms over the steering wheel, her head resting there, eyes right, watching Lyle. It was nearly dark. Five bottles, thrown from a roof, hit the pavement at ten-second intervals. Marina's eyes revealed the faintest clue of amusement.

"A little gasoline, you have a political act."

"As it is, what?"

"Public nuisance," she said.

"Who's the target, I wonder."

"The bottle is the target. They're breaking the bottle."

"That's Zen," he said.

"Whatever works, we try."

"The bottle is the target, master."

"So, Zen, why not?"

Marina was about seven years his senior, Lyle estimated, and was showing today, for the first time, an inclination to be at ease, not quite so rigorous in her convictions, or less disposed, at any rate, to locate every exchange inside an absolute structure.

"Where will J. go?"

"Not far enough," she said. "It's not easy, disappearing, when your previous cover places and routes are closed off to you. J. has no money. He can't have friends, many, anyway, who'd be willing to help him."

"What happens, terrorist discipline?"

She continued to look right at him, saying nothing. This disappointed Lyle. He'd been trying to get her to talk about aspects of Kinnear's situation, past and present. The experiment, as J. had called it, obviously wasn't a case of penetration in the conventional sense. Still, Lyle believed there was an element of premeditation involved. J. had planted himself; he'd infiltrated, at a conscious level, long before he decided to contact Burks or whatever agency it was that Burks repre-

sented. His "selective" disclosure of information merely con-
firmed the material existence of the space he'd chosen to
occupy, the complex geography, points of confluence and
danger. Lyle found these speculations absorbing and hoped
that Marina would provide factual data to round out his concept. Fitting human pieces into gaps on the board. Such activity was thrilling. It was possible Kinnear had been an agent, in
spirit, for twenty years. He'd functioned simultaneously on
two levels. Counterpoise. His life was based on forces tending
to produce equilibrium. Everything had a delayed effect. He
could not act without considering entire sets of implications.
Ended now. Collapsed inward. Possibly he'd worked it that
close to the edge intentionally.

"Is J. homosexual?"

She didn't know.

"Is he likely to turn completely, sign on the dotted line?"

Gesture of indifference.

"Will he be killed, if and when?"

"Forget all doubts."

"Yes, he will be killed."

"It's not an urgent matter," she said. "We have other things
to occupy us."

She moved back from the steering wheel and toward Lyle,
awkwardly, her right leg somehow in the way, preventing the
effect she sought, a forceful intimacy, the exchange of intense
commitments. Finally she put both hands to his face. The
contact was such that it produced a cross-channeling, a lane of
immediate reciprocity. Her eyes were fixed, a little mad—the
wrong effect again. It was interesting, always, being touched
by a woman, the first time, whose mind you know runs on

different lines from your own, who lives by another map, entirely.

"Are we close to something?"

"Getting there," she said.

"Do we have a Vilar?"

"We have someone willing."

"Is it possible he can get instructions from your brother?"

"You mean to prepare."

"Because I'd hate for anything to detonate before it was supposed to."

"Vilar is in total closed confinement. He tried to kill himself several times. They have him under twenty-four-hour surveillance. Vilar will kill himself rather than remain in prison. It's a matter of time, nothing else. It's the act he has rehearsed all his life. Death before pig justice. This is the destiny of one's class."

She returned to her part of the front seat and looked out the side window at the rubble across the street. Three more bottles struck the pavement, about half a block away, again at ten-second intervals.

"But you have someone."

"Definitely."

"He does bombs?"

"He does passports," she said.

It was dark. A group of men and boys stood down at the far corner, laughing. Three of them disengaged and headed up toward the car, teenagers, one holding a bottle between his legs, duck-walking.

"So then I wait."

"Very soon, Lyle."

"We do it the same way, is that it? I let your man come onto the floor as my guest. He leaves the thing. Middle of the night, it goes."

"You two will talk."

"Who is he?"

"Not yet," she said.

"Did you ever dream you'd find another George so easily?"

"It's a quality of Americans."

"What is?"

"Just as Englishmen never cease being schoolboys, Americans are doomed to perform heroic deeds."

"An ironic saying, he interjected," Lyle said.

"Which illness is worse I leave for you to decide."

She was smiling. The three boys passed in front of the car, looking in, and crossed over to the empty lot. She seemed to be waiting for Lyle to get out of the car. A man wearing outsized pants and a T-shirt full of holes approached the car on the driver's side. Marina said something in Spanish. Then she looked at Lyle. The man had recently vomited. Not taking her eyes off Lyle, she said something else and the man walked off.

"The bottle is the target," Lyle said. "I keep telling myself, as a soothing reminder."

"We'll talk soon."

"I'm getting out, is that it?"

"Yes."

"And walking."

"One foot, then the other."

"Maybe you can drop me at Canal Street, if you're going that way, or anywhere near Lower Broadway."

"This is better, right here."

"Or Chinatown," he said. "Maybe you haven't been there lately. Interesting part of the city."

When he got home he emptied the contents of his pockets onto the dresser. Wallet, keys, ballpoint pen, memo pad. Transit tokens on the right side of the dresser. Pennies and other change on the left. He ate a sandwich and took a drink up to the roof. Four elderly people sat at one of the tables. Lyle went over to the parapet. Noise from the streets rose uncertainly tonight, muffled, an underwater density. Air conditioners, buses, taxicabs. Beyond that, something obscure: the nonconnotative tone that appeared to seep out of the streets themselves, that was present even when no traffic moved, the quietest sunups. It was some innate disturbance of low frequency in the grain of the physical city, a ghostly roar. He held his glass out over the edge of the low protective wall. The other people had been silent since he'd appeared on the roof. He dropped the glass from right hand to left. There was that soft fraction of a second when neither hand touched glass. He resolved to do it five more times, extending the distance between hands each time, before allowing himself to go back downstairs.

He was in bed when Kinnear called.

"This has to be brief, Lyle."

"I'm awake, but barely."

"What's your situation?"

"Marina is more or less set on locating you. I don't think she has a clue at the moment as to where you might be, at least that I'm aware of. She still wants to do the Exchange."

"What's your situation, dollars and cents?"

"You need?"

"I'm looking ahead."

"What do you need?"

"Don't know for sure. There are several variables. Just want to determine if you'd be willing to aid and abet."

"I should, what, draw out something now and wait to hear?"

"Draw out fifteen hundred now, good idea, in case the whole thing materializes over the weekend, which could mean trouble getting funds."

"What, U.S. dollars?"

"Good point."

"There's an exchange place near my bank."

"No, stick to U.S."

"Will you be able to change over easily?"

"U.S. will be fine, Lyle."

"Are you in how much of a hurry?"

"Like now, zip."

The next day Lyle was paged on the trading floor and given a telegram, originating locally, with three words on it—NINE ONE FIVE—and the teletyped name DISINFO.

The day after that he experienced what at first he thought might be some variation of déjà vu. He'd finished lunch and stood at the door of a corner restaurant, able to see, at a severe angle, the lean elderly man who frequently appeared outside Federal Hall holding a hand-lettered political placard over his head for the benefit of those gathered on the steps. He, Lyle, was cleaning his fingernails, surreptitiously, using a toothpick he'd taken from a bowl near the cash register inside the restaurant. The paradox of material flowing backward toward itself. In this case there was no illusion involved. He had stood on this spot, not long ago, at this hour of the day, doing precisely what he was doing now, his eyes on the old man, whose body was aligned identically with the edge of a shadow on the façade of the building he faced, his sign held at the same angle, it seemed, the event converted into a dead replica by means of structural impregnation, the mineral replacement of earlier matter. Lyle decided to scatter the ingredients by heading directly toward the man instead of back to the Exchange, as he was certain he'd done the previous time. First he read the back of the sign, the part facing the street, recalling the general tenor. Then he sat on the steps, with roughly a dozen other people, and reached for his cigarettes. Burks was across the street, near the entrance to the Morgan Bank. People were drifting back to work. Lyle smoked a moment, then got up and approached the sign-holder. The strips of wood that steadied the edges of the sign extended six inches below it, giving the man a natural grip. Burks looked unhappy, arms folded across his chest.

"How long have you been doing this?" Lyle said. "Holding this sign?"

The man turned to see who was addressing him.

"Eighteen years."

Sweat ran down his temples, trailing pale outlines on his flushed skin. He wore a suit but no tie. The life inside his eyes had dissolved. He'd made his own space, a world where people were carvings on rock. His right hand jerked briefly. He needed a haircut.

"Where, right here?"

"I moved to here."

"Where were you before?"

"The White House."

"You were in Washington."

"They moved me out of there."

"Who moved you out?"

"Haldeman and Ehrlichman."

"They wouldn't let you stand outside the gate."

"The banks sent word."

Lyle wasn't sure why he'd paused here, talking to this man. Dimly he perceived a strategy. Perhaps he wanted to annoy Burks, who obviously was waiting to talk to him. Putting Burks off to converse with a theoretical enemy of the state pleased him. Another man moved into his line of sight, middle-aged and heavy, a drooping suit, incongruous pair of glasses —modish and overdesigned. Lyle turned, noting Burks had disappeared.

"Why do you hold the sign over your head?"

"People today."

"They want to be dazzled."

"There you are."

Lyle wasn't sure what to do next. Best wait for one of the others to move first. He took a step back in order to study the front of the man's sign, which he'd never actually read until now.

RECENT HISTORY
OF THE WORKERS OF THE WORLD

CIRCA 1850–1920 Workers hands cut off on Congo rubber plantations, not meeting work quotas. Photos in vault Bank of England. Rise of capitalism.

THE INDUSTRIAL AGE   Child labor, accidents, death.
Cruelty = profits. Workers slums Glasgow, New York,
London. Poverty, disease, separation of family. Strikes,
boycotts, etc. = troops, police, injunctions. Bitter harvest
of Ind. Revolution.

MAY 1886   Haymarket Riot, Chicago, protest police
killings of workers, 10 dead, 50 injured, bomb blast,
firing into crowd.

SEPT 1920   Wall St. blast, person or persons unknown, 40
dead, 300 injured, marks remain on wall of J. P. Morgan
Bldg. Grim reminder.

FEB 1934   Artillery fire, Vienna, shelling of workers
homes, 1,000 dead inc. 9 Socialist leaders by hanging/
strangulation. Rise of Nazis. Eve of World War, etc.

There was more in smaller print fitted onto the bottom of
the sign. The overweight man, wilted, handkerchief in hand,
was standing five feet away. Lyle, stepping off the sidewalk,
touched the old man, the sign-holder, as he walked behind
him, putting a hand on the worn cloth that covered his shoulder, briefly, a gesture he didn't understand. Then he accompanied the other man down to Bowling Green, where they sat
on a bench near a woman feeding pigeons.

"How about a name?"

"Burks."

"What Burks? What's Burks supposed to mean?"

The man glanced at a car parked across the street. Burks
sat in the front seat, belted in, looking straight ahead.

"It's generic all of a sudden."

"Do it our way, Lyle."

"I'll live longer."

"I wouldn't go that far, pessimist like me."

"He colors his hair. Kinnear. I forgot to mention it last time. He may have a contact at night court, for whatever it's worth."

"Out of curiosity, Lyle, only, where's he at?"

"Don't you have my phone wired in to the computer that runs the world?"

"Not one bit, to my knowledge, besides which I can't see as it matters because A.J.'s not about to tell you anything too, too important."

"If you don't know, I don't know."

"Suit your own self."

"I might speculate, of course. Make an educated guess. Why don't you tell me something about him first? What you know, whatever. You managed to come up with his name from a voiceprint, apparently, or playing tapes to various people, I would imagine. So what else do you have?"

Burks-2 was spread over half the bench, wiping his fancy glasses with the handkerchief he'd had in his hand the past fifteen minutes. His fatigue, his weight itself, running over, made Lyle relax. He looked like a man who sponsors a women's softball team. He picks his nose with his pinky finger and has sex in automobiles.

"A.J. taught voice and diction, junior college level. He worked part-time for a collection agency. He collected. As a sideline he was involved in prison reform, talking to groups, raising money, state of Nevada. He got radicaler and radicaler, as the saying goes, although what actually transpired in the man's heart of hearts, Lyle, is open to question. There was a little razzle-dazzle in New Orleans, late spring in sixty-three. Hard to get the details straight. Somebody was supposed to get snatched, some lawyer attached to a government committee. He had information somebody wanted. There were connections, funny undercurrents. Oswald, for instance. Cuba, for instance. Missing documents. But seems the thing never got off the ground. Somebody contacted the Justice Department a convenient forty-eight hours before the attempt was scheduled. Old Kinnear disappeared at that point, just about. He resurfaced in Bogotá three years later, where he got to be asshole buddies with some people involved in cocaine traffic. Next thing he disappears and right after that there's arrests by the score. Then we find him on the West Coast with a group of former campus hard rocks and they're in the travel business, running people underground or out of the country. A.J. did a little everything. Not exactly a force in the movement. He's been a courier. He's been a paymaster. As we reconstruct it, he's tried to palm himself off as operational chief of this or that terrorist unit. Wouldn't you think that was dangerous?"

"He may be in Canada."

"In truth, Lyle, I don't care, really, cross my heart. A.J.'s in Limbo, Arkansas, far's I'm concerned. It's out of curiosity, only, I asked. Passing the time."

"He may be in Canada or on his way to Canada. I'm not sure. I could be way off. But I think Canada."

Bread sailed out of the woman's hand and a dozen pigeons came down among the fragments. Burks-1 rolled down his window, yawning. Lyle yawned too, leaning over to read the car's plates.

"We'd like some input on Marina Vilar."

"She still wants to do the Exchange."

"Where's she located at?"

"I don't know. No idea. I think she lives in her goddamn car."

"Who's with her, how many?"

"Don't you know any of this from Vilar?"

"Myself, Lyle, I couldn't tell you if Vilar's a Mexican or a Swede but everything I hear leads me to believe he's ready for the basket-weaving class. A mental. Not adjusting well to present surroundings."

"I only know of one possibility, one other person, and he's probably the one who'll actually assemble the explosive."

"Have a name, does he?"

"Luis Ramirez, maybe. I say maybe. I can't be sure. J. more or less indicated he did passports, he falsified passports. He's spent time with groups in other countries, *if* he exists, *if* that's his name. All three of them may be related one way or another. It's a little confusing."

"Who's J.?"

"Kinnear."

"A.J."

"Your information's a little out of date."

"All three who, the Latins?"

"Right, except they're Swedes."

"I don't see as this is funny."

Burks gave him a number to call as soon as Marina got in touch with him. When someone picked up the phone, he was to give his own phone number and then relate whatever information he had. Everybody was giving him numbers or proposing to give him numbers. He liked it. He had a feel for numbers. He didn't have to write anything down. He'd developed ways to remember, methods that went back to early adolescence. He did it every day on the trading floor, applied these methods. They were secret mnemonic devices. No one else used precisely the same ones. He was certain of that. The formulas were too idiosyncratic, situated too firmly in his own personality, to be duplicated elsewhere.

"Is there a date that sticks in your mind?" Burks said.

"She didn't say when. Not the slightest anything. Don't know what kind of explosive either."

"What's their background, anything?"

"They did something in Brussels once and they did the airport in West Germany—West Berlin, I mean. What's it called?"

"Shit, I don't know."

"Anyway they hit the wrong plane."

"Must have been hell to pay."

"They hit the DC-9."

"What did they hit it with?"

"Rockets."

"Must have been hell to pay back at the office."

Lyle got to his feet. The original Burks responded by starting up the car.

"Aren't you required by law to tell me what organization you're with, exactly?"

"If I had the energy to lift up my foot, Lyle, you'd be required to get kicked in the balls. That's the only requirement in effect right now."

7

On the floor Lyle attended to the strict rationalities of volume and price. Close attention was a benign characteristic, mild eyes everywhere, sanity inhabiting the faces he encountered. This was solid work, clear and sometimes cheerful, old-world in a way, men gathered in a square to take part in verbal exchange, openly, recording figures with pencil stubs, the clerks having to puzzle over handwriting. Paper accumulated underfoot. Secret currents, he thought, recollecting Marina's concept of electronic money. Waves, systems, invisibility, power. He thought: *bip-bip-bip-bip.* A floor broker cuffed him on the side of the head, jokingly, a mock boxing match. Lyle went to the smoking area and called his firm's offices from one of the public booths, asking for Rosemary Moore. When Zeltner answered, he hung up. Frank McKechnie was standing nearby. He smoked with his arms crossed, bouncing on his heels, rapidly. There was an aura about him of manly suffering, things gone so far wrong they could no longer be expressed in coherent verbal form, needing commentary impossible here, tears or shouts.

"Well, then, Frank."

"The world's still turning."

"I see you shaved."

"The outside world."

"It turns, still."

"That much is obvious, even to me."

"It's good that it turns," Lyle said, "or there wouldn't be

this stillness in here. We need that motion, see, exterior flux, to keep us safe and still."

"This is what takes getting used to."

"Because they never told you. Mummy and daddy. Your old pap. You know, flicking his suspenders. Never told you."

"Where do I want to be, Lyle?"

"Inside."

"Correct," McKechnie said.

"About that call I wanted you to make. It doesn't matter. I shouldn't have asked. Everything's taken care of."

"Don't tell me about it."

"It's all okay. Nothing to tell. Finito."

"Because I can't give it my undivided attention, Lyle, you know?"

"It's a religious matter, Frank. Uttering certain words, the names of certain people. It's a deeply personal thing."

"Whatever you're talking about, I agree."

"It touches a nerve in the darkest places."

Already Kinnear seemed very distant in time and space. Lyle's two visits to the gray frame house were spots of fog now, half myth, the living room and yard, the basement arsenal. It was as though he'd overheard descriptions of these areas, never having been there, physically, himself, scratching his ribs, a little dry in the throat. He searched his memory for details of place, a sense of texture and dimension. There wasn't much more than soft-footed Kinnear, his perfect little features and grained hair. Friendly crinkles when he smiled. His voice, mature and professional: two credits, noncompulsory. It was reducing itself, the whole series of events, his own participation, to this one element, J.'s voice, the carrier waves relaying it from some remote location.

He called again that night. When the phone rang Lyle knew
at once it was J. and felt deeply relieved, as if he'd feared
being abandoned to Marina and Burks, to the blunter cate-
gories of reality. Kinnear, speaking without inflection, wasting
not a breath, reminded Lyle that he'd given him a phone
number to use only at his, Kinnear's, specific instruction. This
was to be taken as such instruction and he asked Lyle to make
the call from a public phone booth, using whatever precau-
tions seemed advisable. Before hanging up, he added that the
three-digit number on the telegram Lyle had received was the
area code, digits reversed.

Lyle changed clothes, not knowing quite why. He took a
cab, then walked several blocks to Grand Central. He got four
dollars' worth of silver and stepped into a booth.

"I think we're operational."

"Which means?"

"A two- or three-day holiday, if you can manage."

"Starting when?" Lyle said.

"Day after tomorrow."

"No problem."

"Figure thirty-five hundred dollars."

"What form?"

"There's no limit to the amount of cash you can take across
the border."

"I talked to Burks again. Burks isn't all that interested
anymore. It makes sense, J. They had an informer and they
lost him. They have no reason to be sending dogs."

"It's my ass," Kinnear said.

"Marina, I don't think Marina's capable of finding you.
She's got all she can do to get somebody to put together a
thing that'll make a noise when they light it."

"Lyle, it's my ass."

"True."

"She's capable. Marina's capable. The secret police know my name. They know my background. They'd very much like to chat is my impression."

"I seriously question."

"Are we operational or not?"

"But it's your ass."

"Exactly."

"So how do we do it?"

"Figure thirty-five hundred buys me documents, travel, necessities of life for a while."

"You're not staying."

"Only as long as it takes to buy some paper. The requisite name and numbers. Ever travel by freighter?"

"Then what?"

"For a scuffler like me?"

"You'll be back, I guarantee it."

"Could be, Lyle."

"Burks talked about New Orleans."

"See, told you, they know."

"Not very much, J."

"They spent time on me, those people. They know who and how to scratch, they really do. Goddamn, they mentioned New Orleans, did they? That was how many years ago. Lifetimes is more like it."

"Burks said something interesting."

"What did he say?"

"He said Oswald."

"Did he now?"

"He said Cuba, stolen papers, I don't know."

"They're good," Kinnear said. "They spend time."

"Was Burks saying you knew Oswald before Dallas?"

"Lyle, chrissake, everybody knew Oswald before Dallas."

They both laughed. Lyle turned toward the row of facing booths. Only one was occupied, this by a black woman, middle-aged, in a polka-dot dress.

"Maybe we can talk about it some more."

"Concerning the money, Lyle, I don't know if I'll be able to pay you back."

"No problem."

"Is it a problem? Because if it is, Lyle."

"Forget."

"I shaved it down to the absolute bone. That's the sheer minimum I'll need to get clear of here. Not a dime extra."

They made arrangements. Lyle stepped out of the booth and headed down Lexington. It was late. A car turned toward him as he moved off the curb. The driver braked, a man in his thirties, sitting forward a bit, head tilted toward Lyle, inquisitively, one hand between his thighs, bunching up fabric and everything beneath it. Clearly a presentation was being made. Lyle, who was standing directly under a streetlight, averted his eyes, looking out over the top of the car as if at some compelling sight in a third-story window across the street, until finally the man drove off.

8

Pammy stepped onto the deck. Ethan was still trying to clear his throat, standing at the rail with a mug of coffee. It was bright and warm, already past noon. Jack was at the other end, stacking firewood. Nasal cavities, sinus membranes. She went inside, poured a cup of coffee and returned to the deck, sitting on the rail, head back, her face on a nearly inclined plane.

"But don't you love it?" Jack said. "Every morning it goes on. The exact same thing. As though nobody else was around. Gagging, hawking, the retcher, Mr. Retch. You think he'd do something."

"Get quick relief. Breathe easily, freely."

"Anything, for God, I mean it's, this thing I listen to every morning, *every* morning, nonstop."

"I like to hawk," Ethan said. "It's one of the last great hallmarks of a sensuous human presence on the planet. I like to expel phlegm."

"It's like the subway, two in the morning, you get the pukers."

"No, no."

"You get the dry heavers."

"Hawking is to puking as haiku is to roller derby."

"How can you be talking in the morning?" Pammy said. "Making these things, similarities, analogies, right after getting up, ratios, regardless of how stupid. I can barely open my mouth to drink."

"I like to feel the mucus come unstuck."

She went inside and toasted some bread. Later she walked all the way to Deer Isle village, followed for a quarter of a mile by two large dogs, and bought some postcards and groceries. She was accompanied part of the way back by a girl on a bike, who answered each of Pammy's questions with one or two words before veering onto a bumpy path that led to a pleasant old house. Pammy realized she was smiling at the house, as she'd smiled earlier at the girl and before that at the dogs. She resolved to stop using this cheerful idiot squint.

"Where's Ethan?"

"Stonington, shopping."

"I just shopped."

"He wanted fish things."

"I didn't see him drive past. I guess I was in the market."

"What do you want to do?"

"The meadow?" she said.

"There's nothing to do."

They walked along the beach. Jack was barefoot, treading lightly among the rocks, enduring a certain amount of furtive pain, hunched slightly, hands out away from his sides. He was a bit shorter than Pam, the strength in his shoulders and legs easy to discern in the tank top and denim shorts he wore. She followed him around a large projecting rock, trying to judge the slickness of particular stones as she progressed by tentative leaps from one to another, the tide washing by. They walked another hundred yards to a set of wooden stairs that led up to a broad field, the grass waist-high in places. There was a sign: PRIVATE. It was a pastured square, woods on three sides, the bay to the west. Pammy lay back, undoing her shirt. At this hour sunlight reached nearly every part of the meadow.

"I'm no longer dejected."

"Grass, it stings. It's not like movie grass."

"We forgot the cheese, fruit, chicken, bread and two kinds of wine."

"I used to think grass, a picnic," he said.

"I've been secretly dejected. Now it can be told. I wanted an aggressive suntan. I came here seeking just that. A deep bronze effect. Middle-aged ladies have them sometimes. Like your skin is so parched and bronzed it's almost verging on black. That baked-in look. Like you feel tremendously healthy and good but you resemble this creature, like who's this dug-up thing with the weird wrinkles. I wanted to do that once in my life but fool that I am I didn't realize this would not be the place. So I'm going to relax and get over my dejection and just get what's available, a faint pink tinge."

"Good luck."

"Get into the grass."

"It has things."

"Come on, Laws, sink in, be one, merge."

"Be one with the grass."

"The earth, the ground."

"Earth, creature, touch."

"Blend," she said.

"Air, trees."

"Feel wind."

"Birds, fly, look."

"Wing, beak."

"Sound they make, calling."

"Up in sky."

"Make sound, talk."

"White gull, much air for wings to flap."

"Make fly over broad waters to land of Mamu the bear."

She sat up to take off her sneakers, then undid her jeans, pushed them off with underwear inside them and slid both away with her feet, a well-executed rejection, coming last out of the shirt, which she arranged beneath her before settling back again, arms at her sides. Jack stood up to undress. She liked seeing him against the sky, defined that way, clear and unencumbered, flesh tones a perfect compensation, a wry layered grade, for that extravagant blue. Trite, she thought. Muscled body against sky. Soft-core fascist image, Ethan would say. But what the hell, folks, it's fun to mythologize.

"Getting out of clothes."

"Don't you love it?"

"What is it about getting out of clothes, just stepping out?"

"I know," she said.

She lifted one leg, trying to nick Jack's left testicle with her big toe. He covered up in mock horror, squealing. A light breeze.

They lay side by side, beginning to sweat a little, satisfyingly, as the day reached its warmest point. She raised up on one elbow, watching him. The grass was a problem, itching, digging in.

It was to be a serene event, easefully pleasant sex between friends. The low-grade tension that existed would be released, softly, in a mutual assuagement, a sweetening, clement beyond the edges of its strangeness, the seeming inconsistencies. The child in Jack was what she would seek, the starry innocent, drifting, rootless, given to visions. It was to be a sympathetic event.

She touched his belly with the back of her hand. Jack looked at her carefully, a testing of intentions, a question being put to both their souls, the armature, the supporting core, of their free discretion. He put his hand to her shoulder and moved it down the length of her arm until it met her own hand. He did not guide as much as accompany her.

It became for a time a set of game-playing moods. They scribbled on each other's body. They touched reverently. They investigated with the thoroughness of people trying to offset years of sensory and emotional deprivation. At last, they seemed to be saying, we are allowed to solve this mystery. This was part of the principle of childlikeness that she had sought to establish as their recognized level of perception. With slightly pious curiosity they handled and planed. It was the working-out of a common notion, the make-believe lover. They were deliberate, trying to match the tempo of their mental inventions, hands seeking a plastic consistency.

This interval would pass, these midafternoon abstractions, the mild loving by touch, the surface contact.

Jack sat leaning to one side, left arm giving support, left leg sprawled, the right flexed. Pammy knelt against his haunch, at the deep hollow formed by his hip and upcurved thigh, one hand in his lap, curled there, motionless, the other grazing his head, the back of Jack's head, the patch, the white sign of something, Jack's tribal secret, his meaning, what made him pristine. Posed almost classically on the grass, he kept his face turned from her. Strange, the unnatural whiteness, a pure grade of chalk, it seemed, ground down and mixed with water, the sort of transforming flaw that raises a thing (to be crude, she thought) in price. She rolled her thumb over the area, one inch square, feeling the hair spring back. It was well-trimmed here, of characteristic texture.

He got to his feet and stood over her, cock-proud Jack, bits of dirt and grass stuck to his lower body.

On his back, he put his thumbs to her nipples. His face was reddish and wet and he appeared to be in some middle state, he appeared to be wondering, he appeared to have forgotten something.

Behind him, on their sides, she reached forward and lifted his leg back over hers. There was a small collapse in format and she settled in under him, taking hold, trying to work in, to cancel all distinction between surfaces.

She straddled his chest again, knees inserted in his armpits. She forced his arms closer to his body and dug in, drove with her knees, off-balance, filling, working in, getting tighter, interlocking.

The aspect and character of these body parts, the names, the liquid friction. Dimly she sought phrases for these configurations.

Prone on her own shirt, she felt his hands pressing on her buttocks, redistributing bulk, spreading them to glide his cock along each side of the indentation. Her shirt somehow was the energizing object here. She forced her pelvis up, countering the pressure of his weight, and put her hand under the shirt, lowering her body onto it then, lightly, her left arm providing leverage, the right hand clutching the shirt, bringing a handful up into her crotch. Jack eased off as her legs closed around the shirt and she rolled on her side, knees tucked up, the shirt hanging out of the crease where her legs were joined.

This left and right. Leg, index finger, testicle and breast.

This crossing over. The recomposition of random parts into something self-made. For a time it seemed the essential factors were placement, weight and balance. The meaning of left and right. The transpositions.

Jack, crosslegged, watched. She rubbed the shirt between her thighs repeatedly, knees coming unlocked in the surgical pressure and friction. She opened out toward him, a shade manic, breathing as though in some crosscurrent of exhaustion and need, her eyes empty of intent.

It was no longer an event designed to surprise familiar pleasures. He would cross to her and she would reach out, blankly. They would thread onto each other, her hand at the back of his head. Who were they, stretched this way along each other's length, refitting, going tight, commencing again to function? Her swimmer's body arched against him. Ethan's Jack and Pam. From time to time, weightless, she was able to break through, to study her own involvement, nearly free from panic and the tampering management of her own sense of fitness, of what agrees to observe reason. This lasted but seconds. The rest was dark, a closing over of extraneous themes. She sought release in long tolling strokes. What she felt, the untellable ordeal of this pleasure, would evolve without intervention, a transporting sequence of falling behind and catching up to her own body, its pre-emptive course, its exalted violence of feeling, the replenishments that overwhelm the mortal work of the senses, drenching them in the mysteries of muscles and blood. This ending segment then was "factual," one-track, and she would close, slaked, in a fit of hiccups.

Jack sat in the grass, his eyes following a large bird, cormorant probably, arcing out over the bay. Pammy got dressed, watching Jack, wondering why she was so concerned about him. Did it mean what they'd done had less effect on her than it did on Jack? Did it mean she thought Jack might blab? Did it mean Jack was upset, Jack was already having regrets? Her body was sore nearly everywhere. The earth had hurt. The goddamn ground. She wondered if she'd become too complex to be concerned about someone without listing possible reasons.

"Where's my shoes?"

"You didn't have them."

"I didn't have them, right."

"I speak the truth."

"No shoes," he said.

"Which explains your feet."

"What, cut?"

"Bruised," she said.

He dressed and then started hopping on one foot while he examined the other. Pammy was on one knee, lacing the second sneaker. It seemed too much effort to get up.

"Which way back?"

"I don't know but we should get moving, I guess."

"I guess," he said.

"We say what?"

"We were here, if he asks."

"We took a walk."

"We look, glaa, like a little messy."

"There's a windjammer, look."

"We took a walk to the meadow," he said.

"Can you see it, three masts? Don't worry. We took a walk. That's all."

"Sure, like this."

"So your shirt has a couple of wrinkles. No big deal, Jack."

"Hic*cup,* hic*cup.*"

"Which way?"

"We went to the meadow and what? Looked at some boat for all this time?"

"It's not a problem, Jack."

"Not for you, it's not."

"Look, we skipped rocks for an hour and a half. We looted a graveyard. Who cares? He's not going to question us. We clubbed baby seals for their pelts."

"Ethan is responsible for me. He is willing to be that. He accepts."

"Jack, it's all right."

"I'm in no mood to start things with Ethan right now. He accepts, whatever it is. My whole life. He is willing to be responsible."

She realized she'd had that look on her face, briefly, gazing out at the windjammer, that dumb smile. They headed back through the woods, finding the right dirt road only after a period of some confusion, a brief disagreement over landmarks.

After the rain she sat with Ethan by the fire. At this angle, in his deep chair, he appeared to be asleep. She walked away from the light source and opened a side door just enough to thrust her face out into the night. The force of it, the snap of damp pine, was enough to startle her. Points of bioluminescence were evident nearby, fireflies bouncing on the air, thimblefuls of abdominal light. She noted a faint odor of decomposition, bayside. When she slid the door shut her face grew warm immediately. Awareness washed away in layers and she went back to her chair. Ethan got up just long enough to poke a log apart: rekindling and hiss.

"There's something about your hair tonight. It's very black and shiny. A Japanese quality. The light, the way it hits."

"To go with my German mouth."

"It needs a topknot."

"What's his name, the samurai?"

"You should try that, Ethan. A topknot. Back at the office."

"I do sort of emit a certain feudal menace."

He prolonged the word "feudal." Jack came in then. He took off his sweater and tossed it over the back of a chair. He sat on the flagstone hearth that extended about four feet into the room, his gaze directed between his feet. His voice was subdued, blending suggestions of fatalism and studied weariness. He paused often to take deep breaths.

"I saw it again. Out near the car. There's a gap in the trees. It was right there. I don't know, two hundred yards away. It was the same one. It was pulsing. Maybe not as bright this time. Greenish. The same green. I could see from near the car right out over the bay. Blue-green light. But solid behind it. An object. The light glowed and pulsed so it was hard to tell the shape the thing was. But it was solid. I knew it. I said it to myself standing there. I was carefuler this time. Color, shape, I kept my mind on it. I said don't move, keep it in sight. I never moved my head. I don't remember even blinking. Then it dipped a little and glided up and further out over the bay, going south and west, getting smaller. Then the trees blocked my view and I ran down to the water and I still could see it. Just the light, bluish green, getting small, small, small. Nothing solid. But before that it was solid. I told myself. I said it standing there. This is light from an object. There's a thing out there."

"A turquoise helicopter," Ethan said.

"The way to attack this," Pammy said, "is to make a list of all the rational possibilities. Then see what we can eliminate and what we're left with."

"But no problem. It's a turquoise helicopter. Turquoise is the Maine state color."

"That was a police helicopter."

"Of course. No mystery whatsoever. Patrolling the bay."

"Patrolling the bay for UFOs."

"There've been sightings, I understand."

"I don't care," Jack said.

"And which ties right in with the state motto."

"Turquoise Forever," she said.

"No, In Turquoise We Trust."

"But that's only one rational possibility. We have to list many. Or two at any rate. It's the government standard."

"A turquoise pigeon."

"No, no, come on, has to be different."

"A fourteen-ton turquoise pigeon breathing heavily."

"Go right ahead," Jack said.

"United in Truth, Justice and Turquoise."

"E Pluribus Turquoise."

"There's got to be at least one other possibility," she said. "The man here claims he saw it. It's only right we come up with a second interpretation."

"Saint Elmo's fire."

"What's that?"

"I'm naming the bloody things. Do I have to explain them too?"

"You didn't explain the turquoise helicopter. I knew right away what you meant."

"It's an electrical discharge. A phenomenon that takes place before, during or after storms. I don't know—choose two. See, you people don't know the references. Your early years were abortive, Pammy old kid. I could say a shirt with a Mr. B. collar. You've no idea, right? So-and-so's decked out in his Mr. B. collar."

Jack headed upstairs, reaching for his sweater as he passed the chair, carrying it crumpled, one rust-colored arm brushing the edge of each step as he ascended. It started raining again. Pammy checked a row of paperback books set on a broad shelf between the portable TV and the wall. Mystery, mystery, spy, sex, mystery. The books were old, sepia-toned inside; pages would snap cleanly. Ethan poured a drink and returned to his chair. Proceeding slowly, measuring her steps like an animated toy soldier, heel-walking, she moved to the hearth, sitting where Jack had, a possible token of remorse.

"How upset is he? Is he upset?"

"Jack's whole life he's been made to feel expendable."

"Small things upset him."

"He takes things as accusations, diminishments. Then he in turn accuses, often privately, going off to sulk. I think he condemns his surroundings as much as anything. People he sees within that frame. Some places are good, somehow. Others he feels reduced in. He gets no sense of himself, I suppose. I guess there were places all along the line, earlier. Relatives, so on. The people are blurs now."

"Sometimes you can almost see his mind working. It darts back and forth. You can see he's estimating away in there, working out the advantages."

"Some people have clandestine mentalities."

"It darts."

"Some people are open-natured, generous and humane."

"Us, for instance."

"You and me," he said.

In the middle of the night she heard the trees, that sound of wave action caused by high winds. There was someone in the living room, a fire. She got out of bed. Jack was sitting on the sofa, hands cupped behind his neck. She opened the door a bit wider and tilted her head in a certain way. Conciliation. Permission to enter his presence. He continued to grip his neck as though about to do a sit-up. She sat on the bed. When he passed, half an hour later, on his way upstairs, she was at the door. It was her instinct that touch makes anything possible. The slightest contact. She put her hand to his forearm. Barest touch. Enough, she thought, to restore their afternoon.

"Inside."

"He'll hear."

"Is everything all right?"

"Why wouldn't it be?"

"Jack, inside."

"He'll hear, I said."

"I want you naked."

"Forget, no, we can't."

"He won't know, Jack."

"Where will I be?"

"Jack, let's fuck?"

"Where will I be then?"

Over the next few days she noticed that Jack's sentences never quite ended, the last word or words opening out into a sustained noise that combined elements of suspicion, resentment and protest. This, his New York voice, with variations, effectively replaced the factual near-neutrality he'd established in his report on the UFO.

She went shopping for antiques with Ethan. Jack hadn't wanted to come. To fill this gap she found something to laugh at everywhere, handling stoneware, flint glass with barely suppressed hysteria. Ethan, trying to respond helpfully, stretched one side of his mouth, exposing a gold tooth, and sent air down his nostrils, little sniffles of mirth. When they returned Jack was behind the counter in the kitchen, washing a glass.

"What's in the larder?" Ethan said.

"Lard, that's what the fuck's in the larder—fucking lard."

She watched Jack through binoculars come up along the path from the beach. Tree branches smudged the foreground. She lowered the glasses when he got within earshot.

"Is Mamu the bear angry?" she said.

She listened, in bed, to sounds, weak cries, coming from their room, indistinct whimpers. A car passed on the dirt road. It was getting colder but she was past the point of exercising sufficient will to get out of bed and go over to the closet, where blankets were stacked. She was ten minutes past the point, approximately.

Ethan made a mild joke about the white circles around her eyes, a result of Pammy having left her sunglasses on while lounging on the deck most of the previous afternoon. Jack chimed in. This became the theme that day. White Eyes.

Masked Marvel. Bagels & Lox. She didn't think it was worth a whole day.

When the man at an ice cream stand asked what flavor, she said: "Escargot." Neither Jack nor Ethan laughed. Their turn to team up.

She played tennis with Ethan. He slammed his racket against the mesh fence, refused to answer when she asked if he'd hurt his knee. Pammy was inspired to remember West Fourteenth Street, that smelly gymlike floor, the salving triviality of tap-dancing.

Ethan began using stock phrases to get laughs, the same ones over and over. "Body stocking." "Training bra." "Hostess Twinkies." "Hopatcong, New Jersey." "Starring Maria Montez, Jon Hall and Sabu."

They took the long drive out to Schoodic Point. Jack sat in the back seat, making a birdlike sound, his mouth pursed slightly, upper lip twitching. On a straightaway near Ellsworth, Ethan turned from the wheel and swung his right arm in a wide arc, hitting Jack on the side of the head.

"He knows I hate that sound."

They stood on the stark granite shelving, watching surf beat straight up on impact. The sky to the east was going dark, a huge powdery stir, as of sediment. Ethan made his way down to a point nearer the sea. She couldn't take the wind anymore. It came in stinging and wet, forcing her to adjust her stance occasionally, pit her weight against the prevailing blast. She went back up to the car. About twenty minutes later Jack followed. She could see lobster boats making for home through racks of whitecaps.

"Spray, my God."

"Did you really see it?"

"What?" he said.

"The UFO."

"Twice."

"I believe you."

"I'm going this time. I should have done it years ago. This is no life."

"You keep saying Ethan. Ethan's willing to be responsible for your life."

"Not this time. I'm not saying it, notice. I didn't even mention his name."

Obviously she'd begun to distrust her affection for Ethan and Jack. A place was being hollowed out, an isolated site, and into it would go the shifting allegiances of the past week, the resentments surfacing daily, all the remarks tossed off, minor slights she couldn't seem to forget, and the way they tested each other's vulnerability, the moment-to-moment tong wars. It occurred to her that this was the secret life of their involvement. It had always been there, needing only this period of their extended proximity to reveal itself. Disloyalty, spitefulness, petulance.

She watched Ethan come up over the rail. His nylon windbreaker seemed about to be torn from his chest. The sea was an odd color in places, though beautiful, the whitish green of apples.

It wasn't that bad, really. Close quarters too long. That was all it was. Tong wars, my God. It wasn't nearly that. Everybody's involvement with everybody had a secret life. Misgivings, petty suspicions. Don't be so dramatic, so final. It would fix itself, easily, in weeks. They were friends. She would have them to look forward to again. Aside from the thing with Jack. That might take longer to fix.

Through wailing traffic, a summer of parched machines, she looked across Route 3 to a miniature golf course, catching glimpses of three boys walking over a small rise, shouldering their clubs. It was decided Jack would go looking for a service station, a repairman, a telephone, whichever turned out to be more accessible. Jack didn't favor this arrangement. Jack favored tying a handkerchief to the door handle and waiting for someone to stop. He and Ethan stood behind the car, arguing. Pammy sat on the fender, eyes narrowed against random velocities, the chaos and din of heavy trucks. The boys were meticulous and solemn, measuring out hand spans, precise club lengths, clearly influenced by what they'd seen on television or at the country club. They deliberated endlessly, hunkered down like tribesmen. The course had windmills, covered bridges, all the suspect pleasures of reduced scale. Something about the hour, the late-day haze and traffic fumes, or the vehicles themselves, intervening, some trick of distance made space appear to be compacted, the boys (from Pammy's viewpoint) isolated cleanly from the sprawl around them, the mess of house trailers, tombstones and fast-food outlets. It was near sunset, an antique light falling over the course. She felt she could watch indefinitely, *observe,* without being seen. One of the players reached for his ball, bending from the waist, mechanically, leg up, leg down, an abstract toy. She felt at ease here, fender-sitting, despite the noise and stutter-motion and crude landscape. The voices of her friends edged in at times, piping cries, small against the headlong grieving stream. She had a history of being happy in odd places.

9

Lyle set things out on his dresser. When the phone rang he didn't want to answer it. He'd already fixed in his mind certain time spans. There were boundaries to observe, demarcating shades of behavior. Some faint static could disturb the delicate schedule he'd established, a closed structure of leave-taking and destination.

Driver's license, traveler's checks, credit cards, note pads (2), keys, wrist watch, road map, street map, ballpoint pen, wallet, U.S. dollars (4,000), Canadian dollars (75), cigarettes, matches, chewing gum.

It turned out to be Kinnear, surprisingly. Deprived of all but phonetic value, J. was no less a regulating influence, a control of sorts, providing standards of technique that Lyle was never slow to note. It was a good connection and his voice was warm and persuasive and distinctly pitched, a tone of countless small detonations, as from a stereo speaker, right there at Lyle's ear, reasonable, so close.

"I've been thinking about certain aspects of your involvement, Lyle—i.e., the Exchange, our friend Marina, whatever plan or plans may be in effect. It occurred to me that you mightn't be able to shake loose so very easily. Let me say: don't let it reach the point where either way you turn there's pure void, there's sheer drop-off. You let it get too far, it will literally happen, this business about being George's successor, with the same depressing results. Remember, George thought he was associated with money manipulators, illegal banking

combines. You have the advantage. You also have a clear way
out. I don't have to say more than that. Marina's capable. She
can get the thing to the point where either way you turn,
Lyle."

"I never intended it to get there."

"You saw the basement. George didn't. Take advantage."

"I knew how far."

"These things really go off, Lyle, when they're put together
properly. It accomplishes nothing. It's another media event.
Innocent people dead and mutilated. Toward what end? Pub-
licize the movement, that's all. Media again. They want cov-
erage. Public interest. They want to dramatize."

"I never thought of reaching the point where either way I
turned."

"The whole plan was and is stupid. A lot of ridiculous
theatrics and it's just childishly, stupidly worked out. Imagine
being so lacking in resources and strategies that you have to
base a major operation on this tentative alliance, this weak,
weak, weak relationship with someone who works for the very
entity that's the target and who stands to lose everything and
gain nothing from the whole affair. If there'd been any way I
could have prevented what happened to George, I'd have done
so at any and all cost."

"I'm aware."

"We'll talk more when you get here," Kinnear said. "We'll
talk about New Orleans. Things happened you wouldn't believe. I worked on Camp Street for a while. I'll give you one
guess who came looking for office space at five four four
Camp. His Fair Play for Cuba period. And who kept turning
up at a bar called the Habana. It gets more interesting than

that. Mazes, covert procedures. Strange, strange, strange relationships and links. We'll talk."

Marina, when she picked him up outside the old Fillmore East, 3 p.m., barely looked his way. She drove east, saying nothing. They'd entered a new phase, it appeared. Lyle, in a T-shirt and old trousers, carrying only four or five dollars and no ID but wearing his watch, hung his right arm out the window, feeling drowsy. She parked behind a Mister Softee truck. They walked several blocks and through a vacant lot and then one more block, past milling children and men playing cards at a table on the sidewalk, to a five-story tenement building. A man with a German shepherd sat on the stoop. The dog barked as they approached and the man, shirtless, a huge lump on his shoulder, hooked four fingers onto the animal's collar as Marina and Lyle went past. Another dog, this one in a second-floor apartment, started barking as they mounted the steps. Shat ap. Facking cacksacker. On four, Marina took out a set of keys. They climbed the last flight.

The apartment was furnished sparely. Lyle stood by the window, looking out at a large ailanthus tree. When Marina started speaking he turned toward her and sat on the window sill. There were several cardboard boxes nearby, filled with hub caps and automobile batteries. A yard or so of bright orange material, nylon perhaps, stuck out of a knapsack. A man emerged from the bedroom and walked between Lyle and Marina on his way to the toilet. He was young and moved quickly, making a point of not looking at Lyle as he went by.

"In prison there's nothing that can't drive a person to self-destruction. This is the purpose of jails. Vegetables not cooked right. No TV for twenty-four hours. Things like that are enough. Everything is broken down. All your strength and will. You have to be dependent on the environment to give you an awareness of yourself. But the environment is set up to do just the reverse. The exact reverse."

(It was roughly here that the young man crossed the room.)

"Lyle, we have to be honest. Now if never again. I want you to know about my brother. In his life there has always been an element of madness. I use that word instead of a more clinical one because I don't want to be evasive. I want to give it as forcefully as I can. To those who knew him, there was never any certainty that it wouldn't come at a given moment. Violence, rage, threats of suicide, actual attempts. You had to be prepared to kill him, or love him, or stay away. There was nothing else. Rafael was ready to die. This is the single most important thing about him. Everything around him, all of life, all of people, was an attack on his spirit, his weakness. I witnessed some of this, previews of his death. To be his comrade, or his sister, you had to be willing to accept the obligations that went with it. His behavior, everything he was and did, this was your duty to accept as your own life. He had to know you accepted it. I saw blood more than once."

The toilet flushed. Then the door opened and the man crossed the room again, touching Marina's hand this time as he walked past her. Lyle estimated height and weight.

"It's important to know this about Vilar because in a way everything we're doing here, or about to do, comes from him, originates with his plans, his philosophy of destruction. I've talked of one aspect only. He was brilliant too. He had university degrees, he could discuss ideas in any company. And he could manufacture bombs. He was an angel with explosives."

"And you?"

"I'm less interesting," she said.

"I doubt it."

"I wanted you to hear the truth. In the past I've been guilty of sanctifying my brother. I have no doubt that on the floor of Eleven Wall that day with George, there were elements of self-destruction. About myself, there's little to reveal. I'm determined to use this chance we have. To cause serious damage at the Exchange, at this one place of all places in the world, will be a fantastic moment."

"Attack the idea of their money."

"Do you believe in the value of that?"

"I do, actually. The system. The secret currents. Make it appear a little less inviolable. It's their greatest strength, as you said, or your brother, and to incapacitate it, even briefly, would be to set loose every kind of demon."

"To announce terrible possibilities."

"I believe that," he said.

She called the other man by name, Luis. He stood in the doorway, an elaborate leather band on his wrist. He had the same look Lyle had seen on the faces of a thousand young Latins in New York, boys standing outside supermarkets waiting to deliver groceries, or edging through the rhythmic quake of subways, one car to the next—a secret energy, a second level of knowledge well-nourished by suspicion, and therefore negative and tending to resist, and dangerous. It was present in his eyes, the complex intelligence of street life. You learn to take advantage. You make them pay for being depressed by your existence.

"He wants to use propane."

"I picked up tanks," Luis said. "They're very small. Good size for what we want. I found out about the powders. We have a good mix. Then we add propane in these tanks."

"He wants a fireball."

"When the thing goes, you get a fireball from the propane. Cause more damage that way. All he has to do is get me inside and show me a place to conceal it good. It's exact. I'm making it so it's exact. No loose ends, man."

"How big will the whole thing be?" Lyle said. "You can't walk out on the floor with a shopping bag."

"Hey, I'm telling you. The right size. Just for what we want."

"He has a touch, Luis."

"We'll rip out that place's guts. Hey, you know the sound fire makes when it shoots out of something?"

"Sucking air," Lyle said.

"All he has to do is get me inside."

"Luis has hands. Right, Luis?"

"It's a little different, bombs. I'm taking my time."

"You should see what he does, Lyle. Credit cards, a master. Sometimes he gets moody, though. We're working on that."

"I go to the library. Whatever you want to make, once you know how to use the library, it's right there. I go to Fortieth Street. Science up the ass they got. Technology, all you want."

"Luis has a parachute."

"I wondered."

"Where did you get it? Tell Lyle."

"I stole it in Jersey off some nice lady, she had it in her car."

"Orange and sky blue."

"I saw it sticking it out there," Lyle said.

"A radio and a blanket came with it."

"Common thief," she said.

"A little more time, I would of had the engine block."

"When people come up, he tells them he's with the government. They see the parachute, he says CIA. He tells them he has to keep it nearby, it's in the manual."

"CIA, man."

"The manual has a whole page on how to care for your parachute."

"I say, Hey man I can't go with you tonight if you're taking all those people because then there's no room in the car for my parachute."

"He has to keep it nearby at all times."

"It's in the manual."

Luis stepped out the window and onto the fire escape. Lyle leaned out, watching him climb the metal ladder to the roof. He felt sleepy. Ninety minutes from now he would have to be back at the apartment picking up his things.

"When do we do it?"

"Two days at most we'll be set."

"How old is he?"

"Thirty-two," she said.

"He looks younger, much."

"He's developed a manner. A dozen ways. He's very quick, he slips away. You never know he's gone until you look for him. Don't believe what he says necessarily. He likes to make up a character as he goes along. He doesn't necessarily want you to trust him or respect him. I think he likes to appear a little stupid when he doesn't know someone. It's a strategy."

"He refers to me in the third person."

"His manner."

"Even when he's looking right at me."

"Luis has lived here half his life. To you, he seems one thing. To us, another. Your view of our unit is a special perception. An interpretation, really. You see a certain cross-section from a certain angle. And everything was colored by J., who occupied only a small and routine area of the whole operation. Of course you couldn't know this."

"How many others are there?"

"You know what you have to know."

"No more, no less."

"Obviously," she said.

"A good policy, I guess."

"It's clearly the way."

"Do I believe Luis when he says he's making a bomb by looking things up at the library?"

"I don't think I'd believe that, Lyle, no."

"His manner again. A technique."

"Luis traveled with my brother to Japan and the Middle East. He's acquired a number of skills along the way."

"Plus a parachute."

"The parachute you can believe. I would believe the parachute."

Several minutes passed. The taxed amosphere grew a shade more serene. Lyle moved from the window to a chair nearer Marina. The stress of truth-telling became less pronounced, of performances, strategies, assurances. Luis by leaving didn't hurt matters. He would be careful, Lyle would, not to ask the precise nature of her relationship with Luis. You know only what you have to know. First principle of clandestine life.

"What happens to you?"

"I vanish," he said.

"They'll know he was your guest. You had a visitor that day. You brought him on the floor."

"I'm gone."

"Of course there's another way. No need for Luis to set foot inside the Exchange. You bring the package in. You leave it. This way you can't be identified with a second party."

"Middle of the night, it goes."

"This is cleaner, obviously."

"No second party."

"Think about it," she said.

He studied her face, an instant of small complications. Her eyes measured reference lines, attempting to get a more sensitive bearing on the situation. To the commitment she sought, endlessly, the tacit pledging of one's selfhood, he sensed a faint exception being made. Not all agendas called for rigid adherence to codes. There were other exchanges possible, sweeter mediations.

"J. said you and George."

"True."

"It was part of his least convincing scenario. He told me you'd been to bed with George."

A short time passed. It was decided they would have sex. This happened without words or special emanations. Just the easing sense Marina had loosed into the air of possibilities other than death. She seemed to take it as a condition. Sex: her body for his risk. Not quite a condition, perhaps. Equation would be closer. It was old-fashioned, wasn't it? A little naïve, even. He hadn't seen it that way himself (he didn't know how he saw it, really) but he was satisfied to let her interpretation guide them toward each other.

The bedroom was fairly dark, getting only indirect light. He thought her gravely beautiful, nude. She touched his arm and he recalled a moment in the car when she'd put her hands to his face, bottles hitting the pavement, and the strangeness he felt, the angular force of their differences. Nothing about them was the same or shared. Age, experience, wishes, dreams. They were each other's stark surprise, their histories nowhere coinciding. Lyle realized that until now he hadn't fully understood the critical nature of his involvement, its grievousness. Marina's alien reality, the secrets he would never know, made him see this venture as something more than a speculation.

She had a thick waist, breasts set wide apart. Bulky over all, lacking deft lines, her legs solid, she had a sculptural power about her, an immobile beauty that made him feel oddly inadequate—his leanness, fair skin. It wasn't just the remote tenor of her personality, then, that brought him to the visible edge of what he'd helped assemble, to the pressures and consequences. Her body spoke as well. It was a mystery to him, how these breasts, the juncture of these bared legs, could make him feel more deeply implicated in some plot. Her body was "meaningful" somehow. It had a static intensity, a "seriousness" that Lyle could not interpret. Marina nude. Against this standard, everything else was bland streamlining, a collection of centerfolds, assembly line sylphs shedding their bralettes and teddy pants.

They were both standing, the bed between them. Light from the air shaft, a stray glare, brought a moment of definition to her strong clear face. She was obviously aware of the contemplative interest she'd aroused in him. She put her hands to her breasts, misunderstanding. Not that it mattered. Her body would never be wrong, inexplicable as it was, a body that assimilated his failure to understand it. He nourished her by negative increments. A trick of existence.

She knelt on the edge of the bed. He watched the still divisions her eyes appeared to contain, secret reproductions of Marina herself. He tried helplessly to imagine what she saw, as though to bring to light a presiding truth about himself, some vast assertion of his worth, knowledge accessible only to women whose grammar eluded him. The instant she glanced at his genitals he felt an erection commence.

In bed he remembered the man on the roof. Such things are funny. Trapped in the act of having sex. It exposes one's secret feeling of being involved in something comically shameful. Luis in the doorway with a pump-action shotgun. It's funny. It exposes one's helplessness. He wondered what "pump-action" meant and why he'd thought of it and whether it had multi-level significance.

All this time they were making love. Marina was spacious, psychologically, an elaborate settling presence. At first she moved easily, drawing him in, unwinding him, a steadily deepening concentration of resources, gripping him, segments, small parts, bits of him, dashes and tads. She measured his predispositions. She even struggled a little, attaching him to his own body. How this took place he couldn't have said exactly. Marina seemed to know him. Her eyes were instruments of incredibly knowing softness. At her imperceptible urging he felt himself descend, he felt himself occupy his body. It made such sense, every pelvic stress, the slightest readjustment of some fraction of an inch of flesh. He braced himself, listening to the noises, small clicks and strains, the moist slop of their pectorals in contact. When it ended, massively, in a great shoaling transit, a leap of decompressing force, they whispered in each other's ear, wordlessly, breathing odors and raw heat, small gusts of love.

Lyle dressed quickly, watching her, recumbent, the soft room growing dim about her body. There was a noise on the roof, concussion, someone jumping down from a higher roof or ledge. His hand circled her ankle.

"Does Luis raise pigeons up there or maybe hides explosives in a chimney."

"We get a fireball," she said.

"Whoosh."

He hailed a cab on Avenue C. At the apartment he changed and was out again in fifteen minutes, having already packed. He was well ahead of schedule, as anticipated, and was now operating from an interior travel plan, the scheme within the scheme, something he did as a matter of course when traveling, being a believer in margins, surplus quantities. He rode out to La Guardia, relieved to be clear of the apartment, where he was subject to other people's attempts to communicate. The cabdriver drank soup from a styrofoam cup.

Lyle paid for his ticket, using a credit card, watching as the woman at the console entered various sets of information. He'd thought of traveling under an assumed name but decided there wasn't reason enough and wished to avoid appearing ridiculous to anyone who *might* be interested in his movements. He checked his bag and went looking for a place to get a drink. It was early evening by now and across the runways Manhattan's taller structures were arrayed in fields of fossil resin, that brownish-yellow grit of pre-storm skies. The buildings were remarkable at this distance not so much for boldness, their bright aspiring, as for the raddled emotions they called forth, the amber mood, evoking as they did some of the ache of stunning ruins. Lyle kept patting his body—keys, tickets, cash, et cetera.

He found a cocktail lounge and settled in. The place was absurdly dark, as though to encourage every sort of intimacy, even to strangers groping each other. Airports did this sometimes, gave travelers a purchase on what remained of tangible comforts before their separation from the earth. Piano music issued from a speaker somewhere. Lyle had two drinks, keeping an eye on his watch. Five minutes before boarding he went to a phone booth and dialed the number Burks had given him. To the man who answered he gave his own phone number by way of identification. Then he reported Marina's address and where her car was parked and provided a physical description of Luis (Ramirez) and a general idea of what kind of explosive device he was putting together. The man told Lyle to stay by his phone. They'd be in touch.

The 727 set down at the airport in Toronto. He told the man in the customs booth he was visiting friends—two or three days. Then he rented a car and drove toward the lake, deciding to spend the night at a motel called Green Acres. Looking over one of the maps he'd brought and the street index attached to it, he came across the names Parkside, Bayview, Rosedale, Glenbrook, Forest Hill, Mt. Pleasant, Meadowbrook, Cedarcrest, Thornwood, Oakmount, Brookside,

Beechwood, Ferndale, Woodlawn, Freshmeadow, Crestwood, Pine Ridge, Willowbrook and Greenbriar.

In the morning he drove southwest, about sixty-five miles, to a place called Brantford. He put the car in a parking lot and walked around. Stores, a movie theater or two, a monument of some kind. The town was a near-classic, so naturally secure in its conventions that he suspected J. had chosen it partly for (anti) dramatic effect. Another of his bittersweet maneuvers. To Lyle, enmeshed in a psychology of stealth, Brantford's clean streets and white English-speaking population took on an eerie quality, an overlay of fantasy. It was more familiar than the street he lived on in New York. He'd come all this way, border-crossing, to encounter things he'd known at some collective level, always. Common themes. Ordinary decencies. He could enjoy the joke, even if it was at his expense, more or less, and even if it wasn't a joke.

He crossed a large square and waited outside the modern city hall. About ten minutes after the designated time, he saw a figure half a block away, recognizing the walk, the fluid stride, as familiar, the body itself, familiar, its set of identifying lines and verges. Seconds passed, however, before he realized who it was, coming toward him through a group of children playing a game, that it was Rosemary Moore, her skirt swinging in the breeze. Of course, he thought. Ambiguity, confusion, disinformation. A learning process. Techniques, elaborate strategies.

He decided to offer a warm smile. Took her hand in his. Kissed her cheek. She brushed a lock of hair from her forehead and suggested a place for lunch.

"Just the two of us," he said.

"If that's all right."

"Sure, absolutely, why not."

They walked down a hill to a restaurant called the Iron Horse, a converted train depot. It was dark inside. At the next table four men discussed a shipment of gypsum, speaking the flat language of industrial cultures, a deflated tone, unmodulated, fixed in its stale plane. The waitresses wore trainmen's caps and abbreviated bib outfits. Rosemary took off her sunglasses finally, prompting Lyle to lean toward her, surveying intently.

"Really you, is it?"

"Yes, it is."

"Call me Lyle. Use names."

"I quit my job."

"You quit your job."

"I'll have to find something, I guess."

"Job-hunting."

"I have to see."

"Seeking employment," he said.

"I'd like to get something more interesting this time. I sat at that desk."

"Fly, go back to flying."

"That was awful. You wait on people. I hated it after a while."

It continued through a couple of drinks. He spoke and listened on one level, observing from another. The curiously stirring monotony of it. The liquor and dim lighting. The unvarying sounds from the next table—ladings and capacities. The waitresses coming out of dark pockets on the floor, all

legs, all pussy and ass. The surface context, a landscape un-
accountably familiar, the sanity of a clear afternoon.

"J. wants to know did you have trouble with the money
part."

"No," he said. "But tell him I'm let down, frankly.
Tell J."

"It's a precaution. He couldn't be sure type thing."

"Do I give you the money?"

"If it's all right."

"Can I at least call him?"

"He's not at that number anymore. He's at a different number."

"Have another drink," he said.

"I shouldn't."

"Have another drink."

"If you tell her to make it weak."

"You'll be with J. indefinitely, I take it."

"I don't know. I still have my apartment, at least two
months to go. I may go back and look for a job. I have to
see."

"Do I get to talk to him at all? He said we'd talk."

"He promises."

"He wants me to stay in the area?"

"He said not to go back right away."

"So he'll call."

"You're supposed to give me a number."

"I'll have to find a motel. What happens, you come with
me?"

"All right," she said.

"Did he tell you to do that?"

"Why does it matter?"

"Use names."

"You have to give me the phone."

"He didn't tell you to suggest that, going to a motel with me?"

"He said a number, let him give you a number to reach him at."

"Where is he, nearby?"

She nodded. They smoked awhile in silence and then ordered something to eat. The place had emptied out by the time they finished lunch.

"You've been with him for a while then, I take it."

"I guess, sort of."

"You impress me. I'm impressed."

"Why?"

"One more drink," he said.

"Maybe one."

"He buys a new identity, is that it?"

"He knows someone who can get him whatever he has to have."

"What else?"

"He practices looking different."

"Practices looking different how?"

"In front of a mirror," she said.

"I love it."

"He stretches his mouth. It's gotten so he does it an awful lot lately. It's very macabre if you're walking by."

"Stretching exercises."

"He wants to do his chin next."

They drove half an hour before finding a motel. He checked

the road map, not certain where they were. Rosemary sat on a corner of the bed, handbag in her lap. He had the map spread over a small desk, his back to her, and he was taking off his shirt as he tried to retrace the route they'd taken.

"When do you have to be back?"

"Whenever."

"Where—where we met?"

"Right there is fine."

"Take down the phone number while we're at it. I want to be sure to hear from him. Tell J. that. I was let down. But as long as I hear soon, within a day or two, then that's all right. The money's in a black leather billfold in my jacket. Why don't you count out thirty-five hundred while I'm doing this? Tell J. a day or two. Two at the most. Because I don't know what happens next."

Eventually he turned toward her, beginning to remove the rest of his clothes. He could see himself across the room, angling in and out of view, in the mirror over the dresser. The light coloring. The sandy hair. The spaces in his gaze. It was a body of effortless length, proportional, spared bunching and sags. Nice, the understated precision of his movements, even to the tugging of a sock. And the satisfactions of moderate contours. Of mildness. Hairless chest and limbs. Middling implement of sex. Interesting, his formal apartness. The distance he'd perfected. He could see it clearly, hands and stance, the median weave of coarse hair, gray eyes eventually steadied on themselves.

She went into the bathroom to undress.

He liked motels, their disengaging aspect, the blank autonomy they offered, an exemption from some vague imperative, perhaps the need to verify one's status.

When Rosemary came out, ten minutes later, she had a plastic phallus harnessed to her body.

10

A dog sniffed out hidden riches, circling a grassy patch of earth, again and again, making sure, ascertaining *place*. The gulls were startling, so large at this distance, landing on mounds of garbage, wings beating. She watched them scatter when a second police cruiser pulled up at the edge of the dump. The dog's circles became smaller, more urgent. It was zeroing in, snout down, a little crazy with anticipation. She'd stationed herself at a point where Jack's body was hidden from view by the bulldozer that customarily leveled out the mounds. Smoke rose from charred areas, fitfully. That acrid, acrid smell. She'd stationed herself. She'd chosen carefully. The dog walked off, long gray animal, a corn cob in its mouth.

The gulls stood in garbage, bodies occasionally extended, wings flapping. There were cans of Ajax and Campbell's soup. Maxwell House, Pepsi-Cola, Heinz ketchup, Budweiser. She hated the way gulls walked. They were ugly on the ground, this close, chesty and squat. Burnt garbage. Stinging, bitter, caustic.

Jack was sitting crosslegged. She knew this from the first conditional glimpse. That stump was Jack. While still in the

car she'd taken another look that lasted perhaps two full seconds. His head was slumped forward and black and he was
badly withered. She wouldn't have known it was Jack except
for the note he'd left, telling them where he was, advising them
to be prepared. After that second look she was diligent in
keeping a large object between herself and Jack's body. First
the car and now the bulldozer. He was shriveled and discol-
ored, burned right through, down to muscles, down to ten-
dons, down to nerves, blood vessels, bones. His arms were in
front of him, hands crossed at about the same place his ankles
were crossed. This had seemed ceremonial, the result of research on his part. She *did* think that. She thought fifty different things, all passing through each other, illustrated breezes.
She recalled wondering whether he'd had to exercise will
power to keep his body in that position during the time it took
for the fire to negate all semblance of conscious choice. The
gulls beat their wings, screeching.

She saw Ethan disengage himself from three policemen and
a civilian, this last apparently being the man who operated the
bulldozer. Pammy assumed he'd found the body and called the
police. Ethan walked over to her. He was chewing gum. There
was a strange menace about him, the slackness of his body. He
seemed to be walking right into the ground, getting smaller as
he approached, more dangerous somehow, as though he no
longer possessed the binding force, the degree of concentration, that keeps people from splintering.

"Yeah, it was gasoline," he said. "There's a large tin over
on its side right nearby."

"Burned."

"He set himself on fire."

"He poured it over him."

"Yeah, and lit it."

She held Ethan by the shirt, twisting the fabric in her fists. An ambulance arrived and the gulls scattered again. Ethan looked off into the trees, thinking of something. Not intently, however. He might have been trying to recall the sequence of events in an anecdote. Or something he was supposed to do, perhaps. Some errand or small task. The men were out of the ambulance. Pammy didn't want to think about the mechanics of what happened next or even hear voices in the distance, or sounds, whatever sounds would have to be made. Several gulls started to leave the ground, rising on their scraggy feet, wings rippling, stirring up air. She let go of Ethan's shirt and turned toward the woods, her hands over her ears.

For a while she held her breath. During this period she could hear, or feel, right under each hand, where it covered her ear, a steady pressuring subroar, oceanic space, brain-deadened, her own coiled shell, her chalky encasement for the world of children, all soft things, the indulgent purr of animals sunning. When she let out her breath, the roar was still there. She'd thought the two were related.

She concentrated on objects. Her hands were clasped behind her neck. There was a reason for this but she didn't want to know what it was. She studied the mossy rocks.

It was driving in on her. It was massing. She felt if she untensed her body something irrevocable, something irrevocable and lunatic, something irrevocable, totally mad, would happen. Nothing had a name. She'd declared everything nameless. Everything was compressed into a block. She fought the tendency to supply properties to this block. That would lead to names.

Ethan came back after a while. They walked toward the

car. The ambulance and one of the police cars were gone. He asked her to take his car back to the house. He would go with the policeman. The other man had climbed into the bulldozer and was sitting there, smoking.

"They're very nice. They couldn't have been nicer."

"You'll be gone how long?"

"They'll take me back as soon as we're finished up. Unless you don't want to go there. You can come with us."

"Ethan, what did Jack do?"

"I don't know."

"I mean what did he do?"

At the house she cleaned up. She put things in their original places. She wanted everything to be the way it was when she arrived. The phone rang. It was Lyle. She told him about Jack, beginning a long and at times nearly delirious monologue. She lapsed into accounts of recent dreams. She tried to speak through periods of yawning that were like seizures, some autonomic flux of the nerve apparatus. Lyle calmed her down eventually. He summarized what had happened in short declarative sentences. This seemed to help, breaking the story into coherent segments. It eased the surreal torment, the sense of aberration. To hear the sequence restated intelligibly was at that moment more than a small comfort to her. It supplied a focus, a distinct point into which things might conceivably vanish after a while, chaos and divergences, foes of God.

"Will you be all right?"

"Yes."

"Will Ethan be back soon?"

"I think so."

"It won't be so bad when you're not alone. He'll be there in a little while. And I'll be seeing you very soon. It'll be a little easier when you're back in the city. There'll be people."

"I know."

"Tell Ethan we'll have lunch when he gets back. Call me, tell him. We'll make a lunch date."

"All right."

"Actually I'm not in New York right now. I'm in a motel in a foreign country, believe it or not. Canada anyway. Just a business thing. Nothing special. But I'm leaving right after I hang up. I'll be home in a matter of hours."

"I guess I'll leave tomorrow, depending."

"Don't call the apartment," he said. "I'm not answering the phone for a while."

She had tea waiting when Ethan came back. They sat outside. He wore nothing over his short-sleeved shirt despite the chill. Pammy wondered whether it would be all right to get him a sweater. She decided finally it might be taken as an imposition of sorts, a subtle belittling of his distress. What comfort, really, would warm clothing give him now? It occurred to her that people unconsciously honored the processes of the physical world, danced fatalistically with nature whenever death took someone close to them. She believed Ethan wanted *to feel* what was here. If it rained, he wouldn't move. If she draped a sweater over his shoulders, he might well shrug it off. We are down to eating and sleeping, if that. Rudiments, she thought. Whatever the minimum. That's what we're down to. She watched color spread across the sky beyond the Camden Hills. A sunset is the story of the world's day. They spun back away from it, upended like astronauts, but snug in their seats, night-riding, as the first stars pinched into view.

"They don't have a good burn center here if Jack had lived," he said. "They would have had to rush him to Baltimore, which is ridiculous, considering how remote we are."

"Don't you mean Boston?"

"There's nothing in Boston that's comparable to what's available in Baltimore. They would have had to get him to Bangor first, either there or Bar Harbor. Then on a plane either to Boston or New York, I would imagine. Then from there to Baltimore. So even if he'd lived."

"Ethan, the only thing is time. That's the only thing that can alleviate. Time is change. After a period of time it won't be so bad. That's the only thing you can believe right now. That's what you have to concentrate on. Time will make it easier to bear."

"The consolations of time."

"That's right. That's it. The only thing."

"The healing hand of time."

"Are you making fun?"

"My time is your time."

"Because I don't think this is funny."

"I see myself as an old man," he said. "I hobble to the store for cream cheese and a peach. I buy single items only. One sweet roll, one peach, one bottle of celery tonic. 'How much is that cucumber, young fella? No, the other one.' I stand in a corner of the store and take out my little change purse, seeing if I have enough."

"Stop, really."

"I'm all alone. There's no one to help me shop. I buy stale bread to save money. Kids race between the shopping carts, knocking me off-balance. They barely notice. Their mothers say nothing. I'm practically invisible. I go to a corner of the store and count my change, my few bills, repeatedly folded, folded repeatedly. I buy one onion, a single stick of margarine."

"This could be my father," she said, "which isn't in the least amusing to me."

"Six eggs minimum."

"People live like that."

"I hobble down the wide aisles. My body is too ancient to be offensive. All the odors have gone bland on me. I don't even have the pleasure of smelling myself in bed. They tell me six eggs minimum. I say I'm too weak to break the carton. All I can do is lift one out. Six minimum. That's the rule. I live alone. All my friends are dead, Jack in particular, adorable useless Jack. I stand in a corner of the store and bring up phlegm. I'm very secretive and clever about this. I hawk, secretively. I've learned how to do it so it's not too loud. I feel the phlegm bobbling around at the back of my mouth. I hawk some more. A phlegmy old man. This isn't funny," he said. "I wouldn't laugh if I were you."

She decided not to fly back. It was an eleven-hour bus ride. Watching a small boy come up the aisle to use the toilet, Pammy smiled, close to tears, her face developing cracks around the eyes and becoming lustrous, showing complex regret. The dead elms along the road brought a graver response. She'd never seen them in such numbers, silenced by blight, dark rangy things, their branches arched. It was startling, all this bareness, and the white frame houses, sometimes turreted or capped by a widow's walk, and the people who lived there, how different the dead elms made them seem, more resonant, deepened by experience, a sense about them of having lived through something, although she knew she was projecting this, seeing them only in glimpses, piano teachers (a sign in the window), dealers in pewter and marine antiques. She was eager to be back in the apartment, closed away again, spared the need to react tenderly to things. These were commonplace moments, no more, simple enough to have gone unnoticed at other times. Sloping lawns. A drowsy fern in a bay window. She wanted to be spared these fragments of coastal noon, garbled eyeblinks, so perishable and affecting. And Ethan's strange delineation of the evening before, his deadpan novella. Spared that, too.

So she wasn't unhappy about stepping out onto Eighth Avenue at ten or so in the evening, part of the morbid bazaar that springs up outside the bus terminal every summer night, spreading through the wetness and stench. Restless men sorted among the miscellany. Pigments, styles, dialects, persuasions. Sets of eyes followed her to the corner. Immediately east, west and south were commercial streets, empty and dark now, a ray system of desolation, perhaps a truer necropolis, the outlying zone to which all bleak neon aspires.

Her taxi rocketed east, the back half about to be jettisoned, it seemed. The apartment was serene. Objects sat in pale light, reborn. A wicker basket she'd forgotten they had. A cane chair they'd bought just before she left. Her memory in things.

She couldn't fall asleep. The long ride was still unraveling in her body, tremors and streaks. She turned on the black-and-white TV, the one in the bedroom. An old movie was on, inept and boring, fifties vintage. There was a man, the hero, whose middle-class life was quietly coming apart. First there was his brother, the black sheep, seriously in debt, pursued by grade-B racketeers. Phone calls, meetings, stilted dialogue. Then there was his wife, hospitalized, apparently dying of some disease nobody wanted to talk about. In a series of tediously detailed scenes, she was variously brave, angry, thoughtful and shrill. Pammy couldn't stop watching. The cheapness was magnetic. She experienced a near obliteration of self-awareness. Through blaring commercials for swimming pool manufacturers and computer trainee institutes, she remained in the chair alongside the bed. As the movie grew increasingly maudlin, she became more upset. The bus window had become a TV screen filled with serial grief. The hero's oldest boy began to pass through states of what the doctor called reduced sensibility. He would sit on the floor in a stupor, either unable to speak or refusing to, his limbs immobile. Phone calls from the hero's brother increased. He needed money fast, or else. Another hospital scene. The wife recited from a love letter the hero had written her when they were young.

Pammy was awash with emotion. She tried to fight it off, knowing it was tainted by the artificiality of the movie, its plain awfulness. She felt it surge through her, this billowing woe. Her face acquired a sheen. She ran her right hand over the side of her head, fingers spread wide. Then it came, onrushing, a choppy sobbing release. She sat there, hands curled at her temples, for fifteen minutes, crying, as the wife died, the boy recovered, the brother vowed to regain his self-respect, the hero in his pleated trousers watched his youngest child ride a pony.

Movies did that to people, awful or not. She got up finally and went into the kitchen. Her face looked recently finished,

an outer surface of raw tissue. She supposed she'd been building up to this. There were baffled pleasures everywhere, whole
topographies rearranged to make people react to a mass-
market stimulus. No harm done succumbing to a few bogus
sentiments. She craved a roast beef sandwich, a cold beer.
Nothing here but envelopes of soup.

It was after midnight but there was an all-night delicatessen
around the corner. She got dressed and went downstairs, surprised to find the streets anything but empty. The newsstand
was still doing business, the deli, the bagel noshery, the pizza-
souvlaki joint, the bars, the ice cream store, the hamburger
place. It was still warm and people were in shirtsleeves and
shorts and denims and tank tops and sandals and house slippers. Some elderly men and women sat outside their apartment building in beach chairs, gesturing, munching olives and
nuts. Everyone was eating. Wherever she looked there were
mouths moving, people handling food, passing it around, car-
tons of French fries, sugar cones with double scoops, and talking, hollering, tissue paper drifting in the light air. An average
street. Nowhere special. Not a theater in sight to account for
all these people. All eating. Oral New York. Declaiming
through the slush of mouthfuls of food. Lapping and crunch-
ing. Perennial ranter. The babble king of cities. Pammy had
to stand in line. The counterman licked his mustache and
rolled his eyes.

She emerged with a small bag of groceries. The ghost engines droned everywhere—down sewers, under basement
stairways, in air conditioners and cracks in the pavement. All
these complicated textures. Clownish taxis bearing down.
Sodium-vapor lamps. The city was unreasonably insistent on

its own fibrous beauty, the woven arrangements of decay and genius that raised to one's sensibility a challenge to extend itself. Silhouettes of trees on rooftops. Garbagemen at midnight rimming metal cans along the pavement. And always this brassy demanding, a soul that imposes and burdens and defrauds, half mad, but free with its tribal bounty, sized to immense design.

She walked beneath a flophouse marquee. It read: TRANSIENTS. Something about that word confused her. It took on an abstract tone, as words had done before in her experience (although rarely), subsisting in her mind as language units that had mysteriously evaded the responsibilities of content. Tran-zhents. What it conveyed could not itself be put into words. The functional value had slipped out of its bark somehow and vanished. Pammy stopped walking, turned her body completely and looked once more at the sign. Seconds passed before she grasped its meaning.

The Motel

It's never quite still, is it? Room static. Inherent nuance and hum. And the woman in the bed. Her even breathing. He doesn't know for a fact that she's asleep. He's never seen her sleeping really. He suspects she does it fitfully. Something about her, an aspect of her willingness to carry out designs, to be utilized, suggests a resistance to the implicating riches of deep sleep. He finds it hard to imagine her reaching a final depth, that warm-blooded slumbrous culmination, the point where sleep becomes the tidal life of the unconscious, a state beyond dreaming. To watch a woman at this stage of sleep, throbbing, obviously in touch with mysteries, never fails to worry him a little. They seem at such times to embody a mode of wholeness, an immanence and unit truth, that his feelings aren't equal to.

He's barefoot and shirtless, stretched in a chair. He wears pants with the belt unfastened. The room is dark. He wonders about the tendency of motels to turn things inward. They're a peculiar invention, powerfully abstract. They seem the *idea* of something, still waiting to be expressed fully in concrete form.

Isn't there more, he wants to ask. What's behind it all? It must be the traveler, the motorist, the sojourner himself who provides the edible flesh of this concept. Inwardness spiraling ever deeper. Rationality, analysis, self-realization. He spends a moment imagining that this vast system of nearly identical rooms, worldwide, has been established so that people will have somewhere to be *afraid* on a regular basis. The parings of our various searches. Somewhere to take our fear. He laughs briefly, a nasal burst.

The phone will ring and he will be told to go somewhere. He will be given detailed instructions. The number is known. It has been communicated. Certain assurances have been given. It's just a matter of time. He'll get impatient again, no doubt. He'll resolve to leave. But this time the phone will ring and the voice will give instructions of a detailed nature.

He makes the speech sound *m,* prolonging it, adding a hint of vibrato after a while. Then he laughs again. First light appears, a sense of it, wholly mental perhaps. He doesn't want day to come, particularly. He makes the sound, not moving his lips, expressionless.

We watch him stand by the bed. The woman has made three visits in the two days he's had the room. She's on her stomach now, one arm up on the pillow, the other by her side. Although he's always known her limits, the unvarying sands of her being, he questions whether his own existence is any more entire. Maybe this amounts to an appreciation of sorts. That the lock of bodies should yield a measure of esteem strikes him as incongruous in this case. He notes her paleness. Downy gloss along her lower spine. She knows things. She isn't deadened to the core. She knows his soul, for instance.

(In that moment, wearing her white plastic toy, that odd sardonic moment, so closely bordering on cruelty, a playlet of brute revelation, she let him know it was as an instrument, a toy herself, that she appeared. Dil-do. A child's sleepy murmur. It was as collaborators that they touched, as dreamers in a sea of pallid satisfaction.)

Her complicity makes it possible for him to remain. He stares at the hollows in her buttocks. Dark divide. The ring of flesh that's buried there. We see him walk to the desk, where he gets the map with the street index attached. He takes it to the chair, stretching his frame.

The idea is to organize this emptiness. In the index he sees Briarfield, Hillsview, Woodhaven, Old Mill, Riverhead, Manor Road, Shady Oaks, Lakeside, Highbrook, Sunnydale, Grove Park, Knollwood, Glencrest, Seacliff and Greenvale. He finds these names wonderfully restful. They're a liturgical prayer, a set of moral consolations. A universe structured on such coordinates would have the merits of substance and familiarity. He becomes a little giddy, blinking rapidly, and lets the map slip to the floor.

After a while he takes off his pants. Careful not to disturb the woman, with whom he is not ready to exchange words or looks, he eases onto the bed. Upper body propped by an elbow, he reclines on his side, facing the telephone. Instinct tells him it will shortly ring. He decides to organize his waiting. This will help pull things into a systematic pattern or the illusion of a systematic pattern. Numbers are best for this. He decides to count to one hundred. If the phone doesn't ring at one hundred, his instinct has deceived him, the pattern has cracked, his waiting has opened out to magnitudes of gray space. He will pack and leave. One hundred is the outer margin of his passive assent.

When nothing happens, he lowers the count to fifty. At fifty he will get up, get dressed, put his things together and leave. He counts to fifty. When nothing happens, he lowers the count to twenty-five.

There's a splatter of brightness at one edge of the window. Minutes and inches later, sunlight fills the room. The air is dense with particles. Specks blaze up, a series of energy storms. The angle of light is direct and severe, making the people on the bed appear to us in a special framework, their intrinsic form perceivable apart from the animal glue of physical properties and functions. This is welcome, absolving us of our secret knowledge. The whole room, the motel, is surrendered to this moment of luminous cleansing. Spaces and what they contain no longer account for, mean, serve as examples of, or represent.

The propped figure, for instance, is barely recognizable as male. Shedding capabilities and traits by the second, he can still be described (but quickly) as well-formed, sentient and fair. We know nothing else about him.

About the Author

Don DeLillo is the author of six other novels:
Americana, End Zone, Great Jones Street, Ratner's Star, Running Dog, and *The Names.*
He lives in New York City.